# HOXIE
## FAIR

*Life Before and After*

Copyright © 2023 by Hoxie Fair

**Published By:**
HTF PRINTS

**Book Creation and Design**
DHBonner Virtual Solutions, LLC
www.dhbonner.net

**Cover art** by Moore's Graphics & Designs LLC

**Photography** by Aubrey's Graphic Designs

ISBN for Paperback: 979-8-9882443-1-8
ISBN for Hardcover: 979-8-9882443-0-1
ISBN for eBook: 979-8-9882443-2-5

Printed in the United States of America

# A Special Dedication

There are several people who I would like to dedicate this book. First and foremost, my mother, Ma'Keisha Fair. Thank you for always setting time aside to proofread my books before I release any copies to the public—whether staying up late reading over my material, making sure the grammar is spot on or just giving me insights on what would sound better written another way. You do that so my readers can continue being intrigued and inspired.

Secondly, my aunt Adora Harrison (1993-2023), who was so loving and caring... Even though she battled some personal issues in her life, she never let that stop her from continually reminding me to keep working.

And, last but not least, my brother, Johnny Dean (1991-2023). Over the years, I've learned that the word "family" doesn't have to be obtained by blood but by loyalty and respect. When seeing me out, you always say, "Go home and write a book or something." That's a memory I'll keep with me forever! Although you have gained your entrance into a new world, just know I'll forever be grateful to you. Thank you for pushing me to be great.

THE STREETS DON'T
SHOW LOVE, SO LEARN TO
APPRECIATE THE QUEEN
WHO'S WILLING TO RISK IT
ALL FOR YOU...

# Chapter One

Lamar was a cool, laid-back cat with popularity, money, and good with the women. He often preferred his women to be much older than him. At the age of twelve, he was introduced to crime and drugs. Never forgetting that he was a hustler before anything was what kept him ahead of the game. As time passed, Lamar started to use the name "Lit Red," but how could this young nigga be banging girls with a name like that?

The small town of Delhi where he was from was divided; there was the Hillside, Hall Quarters, Brown Quarters, and then the White Folks Section. Lit Red banged the Hillside and was proud of it every step of the way. He then started getting a team together. But his team differed from all the other hoods in town—Lit Red's team was nothing but hustlers; they took whatever they wanted and whenever. Lit Red was a cocky black youngster. He walked around anywhere, not afraid of a soul. His team members were picked precisely because of the trust issues he had.

His first hustler was a fat, nice-dressing ass nigga named Coop. The motherfucker could eat, lay good dick, and hustle. He had a hell of a combination to say that he was big. Lamar took an interest in him because he was quick on the trigger when getting that paper people owed him. He knew if the fat motherfucker owed him, he would bring his paper back on time. Don't get it twisted, though. Coop was also on the line for six months because Lamar believed in loyalty before anything. Coop was the first member of Lamar's team. So, he earned the title "Captain," eventually becoming Lit Red's right-hand man.

Lit Red had a thing for this girl in school named LaLa, but her parents refused to let her date a gangster like him. The older generation would say things about him, but he wouldn't care. Mrs. Pearl and her Bible study group had conversations about him all the time. "I've lived in this neighborhood over thirty years, and I'm scared to come out my house at times because of that damn mass killer we have walking around here."

"Jesus take the wheel," said Mrs. Pearl.

"You know, I heard that he put a gun to the young lady that sings in the choir father's head."

"Who did, Ms. Shirley?" asked Mrs. Johnson.

"That Lit Red boy."

"Girl, yes… all behind the fact that LaLa's parents won't allow her to date a monster like him. Well, the young fella has always been respectful and showed nothing but gratitude towards me," said Ms. Morgan.

"The little black bastard is a mob leader, and I'm scared to even look at him," Mrs. Pearl replied. "I used to think we had the safest neighborhood in town, but that Lit Red will shoot anyone up no matter who is around him or his target."

The more money Lit Red and his team made, the more the police were paid. Some would even say he had the mayor on his payroll. He was untouchable. He hated when people thought he was a dangerous man just because they feared him. To him, he wasn't dangerous; he just didn't take shit from anybody.

Although Lamar was a hardcore gangster in the streets, he was always on the honor roll in school—often telling Coop that even a gangster ass nigga shouldn't be a dummy. In Lamar's words, "A bread-winning ass nigga can't be slow counting that paper." In school, pussy was offered to Lamar from every direction. He even had teachers pushing up on him, but his attention was entirely on LaLa.

Like Lamar, LaLa was also an honor roll student who often kept to herself. The only other difference between Lamar and LaLa was that LaLa lived in the church house, but Lamar was a street nigga, that got to the bag and caught a body faithfully.

He was so in love with her that when the next Sunday came around, he called Coop at six in the morning and told him to get ready for church. Of course, Coop's fat ass was laid up with some hoe. After hanging up the call with Lamar, Coop thought either he was dreaming or Lamar was losing it for wanting to go to church. It soon dawned on him that the only reason Lamar would go to church was to show LaLa that he was serious and really wanted her. Nevertheless, around 10:30 that next Sunday morning, Lamar was walking up to the church, and so was Coop.

"Look at this good dressing fella," Lamar said.

Coop laughed and said, "Oh, you speaking like them already, huh?" Coop was the type to wear designer from his head to his toes, including undergarments. He always would put on a show when stepping out, no matter the occasion.

Lamar looked at Coop and smiled, letting him know he was still Lit Red. Don't get none of it twisted.

As church began, the pastor had gotten up to speak. The first thing had come out of his mouth was, "What a good God we serve. He even brings the devil to worship at times."

Lamar and Coop glanced over at each other as church members focused their attention on them.

"Man, you sure being here and getting criticized is a good idea," Coop said under his breath.

Lamar looked at Coop in a way, and Coop knew not

to say another word. The preacher opened the service with a prayer. During the prayer, the preacher threw hard blows at Lamar and Coop, saying things like, "Lord, let not a soul in your house be harmed while we are encountered with devilish hearts and souls."

Lamar's blood was boiling, ready to kill the pastor. *Motherfucker, I'ma remind you of a devil when you bring your powder-snorting ass around again,* he thought.

Soon after, LaLa got up to sing, and Lamar's temper began to calm down. It was something about her that made this gangster ass nigga be at ease. As Pastor Mitchell started the sermon, you could tell he had changed his message for the day—focusing on cleaning up the town and taking back the streets. All Pastor Mitchell did was continue to piss Lamar off. Everyone knew that the streets belonged to Lit Red!

Once church ended, Lamar had Coop hold everything down for a few hours; he had some important business to attend to. Being that Coop was his right hand, he was going to do it off the muscle.

Lamar went seventeen miles south of town to a different territory that wasn't his to talk business. When he made it to the location, he saw a slim thick, caramel gangster-ass chick sitting on the porch. As he approached the house, she spoke first. "Damn, Zaddy, that gotta be you."

Lamar blushed while looking at her sexy ass up and down while his dick was getting hard as a rock. He wanted to bend her over instantly but snapped back to reality because he came to talk business. Emphasizing one of his favorite mottos, "Money over bitches."

The sexy ass lady told Lamar, "Come on, Zaddy... let's go in and talk."

Lamar followed her in, constantly watching her ass as she led the way. She offered him a drink, which he promptly declined. He knew her as a hustler but never knew her name. Word on the street was that she was calling big girl shots and making hella bread. That alone made Lamar make calls to set up a business encounter with her.

She soon introduced herself. "My name is Nicole, but in the streets, they call me Nikki... and I'm well respected." When Lamar asked her age and what she could bring to the table, she said, "I'm twenty-four. And I have financial resources, and dope connects to bring my own table. Don't let the good looks fool ya." She was then only waiting to be a part of the team.

Lamar smiled and told her, "Welcome aboard."

"Thank you, Zaddy," she replied, smiling back.

Lamar knew that on that Sunday evening, he had made a wise choice about this new team member. He drove back to town and saw Coop grinning in a known hoe's face. Pulling up, he said, "Man, you gotta stop that shit; them nasty hoes gon' get you out of all your money."

"Bro, no, they won't... I can promise you that."

"Yeah, man, I hear you," Lamar said. "Keep on. Nikki gonna be a captain."

"Nikki?!" Who is Nikki?" Coop asked.

"The new member of the team nigga, and she about her paper," Lamar replied.

"Why didn't you get my opinion of the bitch first?"

"Last time I checked motherfucker, this my shit. So, I make the decisions," Lamar said, laughing as the two went their separate ways.

\* \* \*

A few days had passed, and Lamar had only spoken to Coop about business, which was a strange vibe. Coop soon approached Lamar that Wednesday.

"What's going on?" he asked.

"Stay tuned, my nigga...."

# Chapter Two

It was a Friday night, and the local spot on the rise called "The Little Den" was the spot to be for every teen in the surrounding area. Lamar was doing his thing in the middle of the dance floor, while Coop had been flirting with every hoe in sight—flashing money and shit —like a boss. He didn't know Lamar had already told Nikki to come through. Because he had not yet met her, he thought she was another ordinary hoe when she and her girls walked in.

"Bro, look at this chick," Coop remarked. "It's a must that I fuck her... even if I have to pay for it."

Lamar turned and looked, then began laughing. "Every female isn't impressed or interested with money all the time, ole trifling ass nigga."

Nikki walked right up to Lamar and said, "Lilrdze Gutta Zaddy," and kissed him on the cheek.

9

The look on Coop's face was like a baby who had just dropped his bottle and couldn't pick it back up. After a speechless moment, he said, "Wait... what the fuck you just call him?"

Nikki repeated herself. "Lilrdze Gutta Zaddy."

When Coop saw Lamar's expression and confirmation smile, he knew his boss had changed the game.

"Nikki, this is my boy, Coop. Big man, this is Nikki."

"So, wait," Coop said. "This the other team member you spoke of?"

"Yes, I am, Lil Baby," Nikki replied, smiling.

Of course, Coop's ass went on with his move. "Well, the first thing I need to do being team captain is talk to you alone."

Nikki nodded and walked with Coop back outside.

"Well... I need to see firsthand is the pussy straight," Coop said, licking his lips.

Nikki laughed. "Lil Baby, whenever our boss get it, ask *him* how good it is."

"Our boss...?"

"Yes. *Our* boss," Nikki replied. "The same nigga you take money to is the same nigga I bring money to."

Coop walked back into the building. You could tell that he was mad about the conversation. Nikki came in behind him a few minutes later, making niggas not even care about their relationships or whatever Shawty they were with; they were strictly focused on her. She had bronze skin, the most beautiful face you'd ever seen, and the body of a goddess: her snatched waist, nicely set up breasts, and full hips and ass made all heads turn, including the females.

Nikki approached Lilrdze and said, "Zaddy, tomorrow night, my house... nine sharp. Don't be late."

"What about me?" Coop asked.

"What about you?" Nikki answered. "What I just tell you outside, Lil Baby?"

"Oh, okay," Coop replied, slowly walking away.

\* \* \*

Later that night, Lamar and Coop went to IHOP to eat, where there would be a massive shootout later. Word on the street was that it was all behind rumors that Lamar had taken over a territory that wasn't his, and the niggas wanted their shit back. Lamar would rather die before he gave anything back. It was four in the morning when Nikki heard the news. But, she didn't worry because she knew her boss was a gangster-ass breadwinning nigga.

Around nine that following morning, Lilrdze and his team were in motion— working every block and stacking paper. There wasn't a drug around that the team didn't have. Later that day, a FedEx truck dropped off a package labeled "fragile" for Lamar.

Lamar looked at Coop and said, "Man, I should've ordered you a fashion ink t-shirt," before opening the package and handing him a box.

Coop took the box, opened it, and pulled out a diamond chain that included a pendant with crushed stones spelling out "Y.I.C." Happy to represent the brand, Coop said, "Man, we got these chains now... I feel important."

"*Youngins in Charge* is a family. No more of that team shit," Lamar replied.

Around seven that evening, Lamar told Coop to hold it down because he needed to go home and get ready.

"Nigga, where you going?" Coop asked.

"Nigga, you were there when Nikki told me to swing through!"

Coop laughed and said, "Let me know how it is, boss."

But Lamar was lost trying to figure out what the hell Coop was talking about.

On the way to Nikki's house, Lamar was curious about what she wanted. But as soon as he pulled up, he saw candles lining the sidewalk. As he went to the door, rose petals were everywhere, spelling out "Come on in."

The gangster in Lamar left for a second but quickly kicked right back in, and he took a moment to change the magazine in his gun from the standard clip to an extended one. But when he opened the door, candles and incense were laid out around the house, leading

into the bedroom where soft R&B music was playing....
and Nikki was standing in the midst of it all, dressed in
blue lace lingerie since she knew that Lamar banged
blue.

The young nigga was speechless. "What's the occasion?" he asked, lowering his gun.

"To show you my loyalty, Zaddy. I just need a little of
your time."Nikki didn't waste any time. After leading him
to the bedroom, she immediately took his pants off and
started sucking Lamar's dick, caressing his balls gently
with her hands like she was in a video. Before he could
say anything, the young nigga was moaning out loud.
That was all Nikki needed to hear. She started wildly
stroking her pussy, while all her juices flowed tremen-
dously. Lamar erupted in Nikki's mouth, then began
fucking her, thrusting his dick deep inside her as she
moaned softly.

Once they both reached their climax, they rolled
over, dripping with sweat. Nikki had seduced her boss so
much that she fucked him raw. Lamar had come with
two condoms and would also be leaving with them. Being
caught up in the moment, he flooded her tight, wet pussy,
which made him nut in her about four times.

Usually, when Lamar would go somewhere, he would
call Coop, no matter what time it was, to let him know he
had made it back home. But this night was different —
Coop didn't receive a call from his boss. So, at about five
that next morning, Coop decided to call Lamar. When

Lamar answered, Coop could tell that Lamar was still asleep.

"Damn, boss... Man, you good? You safe?"

"Yeah, son," Lamar replied sleepily. "I'm good. I fell asleep at Nikki's."

After the two hung up, Lamar got up. Even after a great time with Nikki, Lamar hadn't forgotten about attending church to see LaLa. As he rose, he realized Nikki's pussy juice was still all over his dick. He woke Nikki up, saying, "Nikki, I got to go, and it's about time for you to get up and get your day started as well."

"Yes, Daddy," she groggily replied, slowly moving down to slurp some more on her boss' dick before he could get out of bed.

Afterward, Lamar dressed and headed to the door as Nikki followed him and watched him get into his Mercedes Benz E350. Pulling off, Lamar received a text that said: *Thanks, boss. Until next time.*

# Chapter Three

The streets of Delhi were taken over by Lamar and his crew. Nikki had her town on lock, but that wasn't enough for the young hustlers.

After school that Monday afternoon, Y.I.C. was locked and loaded to head to a small town named Rayville. Again, everybody knew not to play with the young monster; he knew where the major drug dealers stayed. When Lamar and Y.I.C. pulled up to a big brick house, he signaled directions to his soldiers, and they knew exactly what to do. Lamar had such a brave heart. He opened the door to the house and walked right in.

"Whoever you are, you better have a good fucking reason for walking into my house uninvited, my nigga!"

"I don't want no problems, my man," Lamar responded. "I just want to talk."

The big black fucker who had spoken dropped his

PS4 controller, and before he could reach for his gun and turn around, Nikki was already standing in front of him with the A.K. in his face.

"What's up, Papi?"

Coop came from the back of the house and threw the hustler's wife onto the floor. From there, Lamar took over.

"William Tank Smith, thirty-seven years old, been a Rayville native all your life. You have four hustlers who work for you. You have a beautiful wife with two kids. I must admit you have a nice crib here, my brother. You also have a Benz, while your wife drives a GL450," he said.

"How in the fuck do you know all this?" Smitty asked.

Nikki hit him in the gut with the butt of the A.K. "Let him finish.!"

"I like the way you hustle," Lamar continued. "But now you going to do it my way... and before you say anything, listen closely. You're either going to work for me and keep money coming in and product moving, or you're not gon' work at all. Now, before answering, think about what choice you about to make."

"Little young nigga! Do you not know who I am and what I'm capable of?"

"See, William... I thought you was smarter than that. I really did. But see, nigga. I don't give a fuck about who you are and what you think you can do," Lamar said.

"So, I'll ask you this for the last time... are you going to provide for your family or not?"

Smitty looked over at his wife before responding. "You think I'm about to work for you? Nigga, you my son's age... so FUCK NO!"

Lamar smiled. "Coop, shoot this motherfucker to show him I mean business."

Coop grabbed Smitty's wife, Jasmine— a model type with gorgeous skin and a Coke bottle figure—by her hair and told him to look. He turned away, but Nikki hit his ass again with the butt end of the gun, making him look as Coop shoved his dick down his wife's throat at gunpoint. Coop was just as vicious as his boss. He ordered her to say his name, and she muttered, "Daddy."

"Okay, man," Smitty pleaded. "I get you're serious. But leave my family alone... please, man!"

Lamar looked at Coop enjoying Jasmine's mouth, and told him to wrap it up. Coop told her to stop, but she started kissing his dick and saying, "Yes, Daddy!" Coop's crazy ass had Nikki and Lamar cracking up when the fat motherfucker blurted out, "Oooweee, I like this respectful hoe."

Once Lamar got Smitty's agreement that he would now work for Y.I.C., Lamar threw him a bag containing a shirt and products, said, "Welcome aboard," and walked off — stating that he would be in touch.

"Welcome to Y.I.C., Lil baby," Nikki said before shutting the door.

When the three of them had made it back outside, Lamar told everyone to load up and follow him. He then went to each of Smitty's blocks, telling the workers they worked for him now.

"If anything happens, call my number... no matter what time of the night," he said. And they knew that Lamar meant business.

By the time the day had ended, Lamar had Rayville, Winnsboro, and Delhi covered, and there wasn't a soul who could stop him or Y.I.C.

* * *

A couple of days later, Lamar was about to head in, but a strange feeling flooded his body. As he got into his car, the sheriff came down and held him at gunpoint. Luckily, Lamar had nothing on him but $7,200 in cash. At seventeen—and a month away from high school graduation—he was considered an adult in Louisiana and labeled as a mob boss of Northeast Louisiana on the 10 o'clock news.

When Coop got the news, he called Ms. Carroll. "Lamar pays a monthly $500 retainer to a lawyer for each member of our crew for situations like this. Call him, and you won't have any worries," he said, giving her the number.

Minutes later, a secretary was answering a phone call. "Sveirman's Law Firm." Ms. Carroll figured that Coop had given her the wrong number because it cost at least ten thousand dollars or more to even talk to a paralegal at Sveirman's Law Firm. "I was told to call you because my son has been arrested," she said to the voice on the phone.

The secretary asked for the client's name.

"Lamar Carroll," she answered before being placed on hold.

After a brief moment, another voice spoke, but it was a man this time. "Ms. Carroll," he said. "You have nothing to worry about... just tell me where he is, and I'm on my way."

"He's being held at the Richlend Parish Detention Center on a $27K bail, and I don't have that type of money, Sir..."

"I assure within the next few hours, your son will be home," Mr. Sveirman replied. "You have my word on that."

\* \* \*

Nikki was worried sick about her boss, not knowing what would happen. After she talked to Lamar and smoked a fat ass Kush blunt, she was soon okay.

Upon Lamar's return to school, he was considered armed and dangerous by the police, but they couldn't find anything to charge him with for the murder of a well-known activist in the community.

# Chapter Four

A month passed, and the Y.I.C. was hustling so hard and strong that Lamar decided to reward them. A weekend had finally come available, so he took Coop, some unknown hoe of his, Nikki, Smitty, and Jasmine, to Dallas to enjoy themselves. They went out of town presidential style—in a Mercedes Benz Sprinter with a paid driver—staying in a $434 per night five-star hotel.

Lamar had a talk with them while they were on the road, telling them how proud he was of the hard work and money the crew was putting in. Only Nikki and Smitty had their own crews made of young, hungry hustlers.

While checking into the hotel, Nikki started getting sick, vomiting everywhere. She really didn't know what was going on. So, after settling into her room, she texted her boss, letting him know she was about to lie down and nap because she wasn't feeling her best. Lamar considered going over to comfort her, but it was only a fleeting thought.

Later that night, everyone was dressed in their finest, ready to explore the city. A woman that Lamar used to date in grade school stayed seven miles from his hotel, so when he called her, she came through. She was dark-skinned, slim, and tall with a petite body but thick as fuck. As she and Lamar made their way downstairs to the lobby to meet up with everyone else, they looked into the mirror of the elevator, saw they were matching, and began to smile.

When Lamar introduced Shanterrica to the team, Coop smiled as he remembered cheating off Shanterrica's tests in school. But Nikki wasn't smiling. Instead, she headed to exit the doors, looking like she wanted to kill this female because it was supposed to be her in that spot.

The young hustler took the fam to a strip club named Purity City. He was such a boss that he didn't even get checked for I.D. and was laid back off in the V.I.P. section getting bottle after bottle sent for free. But, the only way Nikki could enjoy herself was by spending money. She blew at least three bands that night on some of the hottest hoes in town—even had one eat her out.

As the night began to wind down, Lamar knew he wasn't going to leave town without having Shanterrica. Once they had made their way back to the hotel, he took her to his room, where she told him that she needed to use the bathroom. The suite was so big that Lamar couldn't hear the water running in the shower... he was sitting in the front room when Shanterrica came out in a bathrobe. R. Kelly's song "Bump N Grind" started to play as she dimmed the lights, but Lamar acted as if he didn't know what was going on when. Shanterrica slowly walked over to Lamar, kissed his neck, and then sat her thick thighs on his lap.

Meanwhile, Nikki was thinking about how she had been behaving. Snapping back to reality, she began to act like the Boss Bitch she was. Going to the driver's room, she wanted him to take her to the nearest pharmacy they could find. Since the driver was being paid, whether asleep or driving, he got up, dressed, and took her to a nearby Walgreens.

Nikki went in and asked the pharmacist for the top-selling pregnancy test. Three tests were recommended. Leaving the drugstore, she felt in her heart that she might be pregnant because she had missed her monthly cycle. After sliding back into the sprinter, Nikki started to cry again, trying to hide the fact that she had caught feelings for Lamar. As they pulled back up to the hotel, she instructed the driver to tell everyone not to bother her until after 3 pm. Nikki was so damn fine the driver watched her walk into the hotel and mumbled to himself, "If only I were younger."

In Lamar's room, Shanterrica slipped into a neon pink glow-in-the-dark lingerie set she had purchased earlier that day. Lamar watched as she danced to Beyonce's song "Dance For You." With her ass going up and down, it felt like he had brought a stripper back to his room. Shanterrica pulled the thong up by her teeth, showing Lamar all her pinkness. As Lamar viewed her pretty pink pussy, he spoke just loud enough for her to hear over the music.

"Was it all worth the wait?"

Grinning slyly, Shanterrica reached into his pocket, grabbed a condom, and told him to go to work. As they started in the living room, Shanterrica moaned, "Lil Red," out loud.

Lamar was still beating Shanterrica's pussy out as Nikki exited the elevator and walked to his room. Outside the door, all she could hear was, "Zaddy, I fucking love you, Lil Red. Fuck me!" Turning and heading to her room, tears slowly ran down Nikki's face, but when she got to the other side of the door to her suite, she wrapped herself in the covers of the king-size bed and cried like a baby.

The following morning, the team headed out for brunch. Smitty noticed that Nikki wasn't in the sprinter. So, the driver told Lamar that she had asked not to be disturbed until after three.

"Did she seem to have a problem when you last saw her?" Lamar asked.

The driver told him that she came to his room last night and asked to be taken to the store. Lamar started to wonder, then simply said, "Okay."

"We went to a Walgreens," the driver continued. "She came out with a bag, and as we were headed back to the room, she started to cry."

"Did she ever say what was going on?"

"No..."

Momentarily glancing toward the hotel door, Lamar told him to pull off. He was beginning to worry about Nikki, so he texted her to see if everything was okay and genuinely checked on her, but he never received a response. Then, while at brunch, Lamar barely touched his food. Smitty or Coop had never seen him worried the way he was. Even Shanterrica did everything in her power to cheer him up, taking him to the sprinter and filling her mouth up with his dick and cum. But nothing was helping; even though Shanterrica's head was damn good, he was still down.

It was approaching one o'clock that afternoon when Nikki finally got up to start her day. She looked down at the Walgreens bag, took it into the bathroom, and decided to take all three tests. Her phone started to ring, but she wanted to see the test results first. But, after missing that first call, it rang again, so she stepped back into the bedroom and grabbed her phone. "I'm busy. I'll call you back," was all she said before disconnecting the call and rushing back into the bathroom.

Lamar was immediately furious.

Picking up the test sticks one by one, Nikki couldn't believe it. Then, smiling, she turned on the shower, knowing she'd be a mother in less than nine months. After showering, drying off, and putting lotion all over her body, Nikki proceeded to the bed and began to penetrate her fat wet pussy with her vibrator—getting into it more and more by the second. That's when she looked up and, seeing Lamar looking at her, instantly climaxed.

"Lamar, what are you doing here... why didn't you knock?!"

"I wanted to know why you been ignoring me all morning."

Sitting up and pulling on her bathrobe, Nikki sighed. "I've been sleeping and feeling kind of sick, so I turned my phone on "Do Not Disturb" until I was up."

Lamar looked at Nikki momentarily and then said, "Get dressed. We about to head out."

* * *

The Y.I.C. went to pick up the customized chains and pendants from Johnny Dang Company which hit for fifty-two bands, which was nothing to a boss like Lamar. Coop had stepped out of the sprinter to answer a call to learn that a known smoker was spotted talking to police, pointing at their spot. After he told Lamar the news, the team returned to the hotel, got their luggage, and hit the highway to deal with the problem. Lamar sent Shanter-rica a text telling her he would fly her out to him in a week or so. She understood because she knew who she was dealing with.

Upon their return to town, Lamar and Coop rolled up on the smoker and threw him in the car. Coop drove as Lamar talked.

"What the fuck was you pointing out one of my spots for?"

"The sheriff paid me two hundred dollars to show him where I got my drugs from," the smoker replied.

Lamar then made it clear that anyone interfering with his money would be escorted off the face of the earth. "That mistake just cost you your life!"

The smoker's eyes opened wider than a bag of chips because he knew they weren't playing with him.

The last thing he heard before a bullet whipped through his head was Lamar telling Coop to burn the truck and get back to work while he determined their next move.

# Chapter Five

Graduation was approaching, but Lamar knew that he had to do a bid, but he wasn't going to be gone very long. It was a Tuesday morning, Lamar was sitting in class, and the teacher had asked the students about their graduation plans. LaLa shared that she was going to college to become a lawyer, and Lamar knew she had the brain to do so. When it was his turn to speak, the teacher and class were surprised by his response.

"I want to become a surgeon that saves lives."

The classroom was so quiet that you could hear the traffic on the highway outside.

Coming up on third period, Lamar finally caught up with LaLa by herself and went with his move. When he approached her, he immediately opened up to her. "I know I'm not who your parents would want you to be with, but I'm not the person they portray me as either.

Sure, I've done wrong and made mistakes, but at the end of the day, I'm not a monster. I came to you as a man and explained all of this face to face."

LaLa looked at Lamar and said, "I never cared about what the media had to say about you. I only cared about the way you handled your business. You are too smart for that, Lamar..."

Lamar slowly shook his head as they went their separate ways, accepting what LaLa said. Because deep down inside, he knew she was right.

*   *   *

Lamar was part of a small senior class that included 63 students. For the last day of school, he catered food for the entire graduating body and their teachers. He also gave every student a $100 bill.

Almost done with high school, Lamar felt a weight lifted from his shoulders. Aside from the ceremony, one thing was left to complete before he could move on. When he went to see his attorney, Lamar knew what consequences he faced. Walking confidently, he went directly into Mr. Sveirman's office, and the two men got straight to business.

"It was hard fighting this case, but the longest you will be gone will be six months," the attorney stated.

Lamar dropped his head. "Well, Mr. Sveirman, graduation is on Tuesday, so I will turn myself in Wednesday. We can get the process started."

After leaving the lawyer's office, Lamar called Coop to meet up. While pulling up, Lamar saw Coop serving Pastor Mitchell. By the look in Lamar's eyes, Pastor Mitchell knew he had fucked up. Lamar slammed his car door, and it went from there. "How could you call us the devil, and you filling your motherfucking head and nose up with coke!"

"Well, Lamar... you know I have to give the congregation what they want. That's what makes me a good pastor."

"Motherfucker," Lamar roared. "I don't give a damn if you're trying to keep your mama happy. If you ever fix your fucking lips to speak on me again, your congregation will be viewing your body."

"I think he gets the picture," Lamar said, chuckling. "This sorry motherfucker has pissed his pants!"

"Now get the fuck out my face," Lamar continued as he lowered his gun.

While Lamar handled business with his attorney, Nikki handled her business at the doctor's office. After discovering that she was pregnant, she carried herself differently than usual. There was a better reason to hustle and another reason to smile. Since Nikki hadn't told Lamar she was pregnant, she took herself to the doctor and acted as if she was single.

"Are you still having intercourse with the father?" Dr. Lukewiski asked.

Nikki was immediately speechless as her eyes watered up, so the doctor knew he had hit a sensitive spot.

After the examination was complete and Nikki had left the clinic, she received a group text from Lamar, telling the team to meet up at his spot in his town.

As he was new to everything, Smitty had never gotten a text like that from Lamar. Reflecting on the day Lamar invaded his house, he could only imagine what would happen to the next hustler's territory. He only would say, "Load up and follow me."

Y.I.C. hit I-20 and headed east as their boss led them. They drove twenty miles, then got off on Tallulah. At the exit, a second group text came in from Lamar saying that they were going in with extended clips. Nikki held a 100-round drum, Coop had two 34-round clips, Smitty carried two revolvers, and the boss carried 34 rounds. Lamar and Y.I.C. pulled up to a gated house with cameras all around and dogs barking at each side.

Coop, being the loyal captain that he is, drove his truck through the fence and let the team proceed to make their entrance. You would've thought that cavalry hit Neiko's house the way they entered it. Lamar never tried to hide the fact that he was coming for you. When it was time, he came as is.

Neiko was a big-time Kush mover who was moving twenty-five pounds or more per week, but he was yet to be introduced to Lamar. Neiko had hoes and money, but he wasn't the flashy type. Neiko had been sound asleep when Y.I.C. raided his house, and now jolted awake, he found himself looking directly into the sights of two revolvers.

"What's going on?" Neiko asked.

Smitty spoke first. "You know what this is, nigga. You either rolling with us or you dead."

Neiko acted as if he didn't understand, so Smitty dragged his ass into the front room where Lamar was sitting on the couch, making himself at home.

"Could somebody tell me what's going on and why the fuck are y'all in my house..." Neiko exclaimed, in total disbelief about what was happening.

"It's simple," Lamar said. "You see, with me, fella... you can cut the tough guy act. I know everything about you already."

"This a nice ass spot for a nigga that only details cars," Coop remarked.

Neiko had pictures of him and his detailing business posted on his walls, but Lamar knew it was a cover-up to what was actually real. Lamar then explained to Neiko that he no longer worked for himself and now moved product for him. "Do you understand?" Lamar asked.

Neiko was so scared that he simply nodded and accepted the offer on the first plea. As they were leaving,

Lamar told Neiko, "You'll be getting a call from me soon. Stay up, cold world." Neiko couldn't believe what had just happened, but he knew from how Lamar was rolling that he meant business.

After returning to their vehicles, Lamar told the team to return to their cities and check all their spots. The run-in with the feds had him spooked.

* * *

Saturday had come, and Lamar and Coop were four days away from graduation. Coop insisted that they fly out to Cali to chill for a week, unaware Lamar was leaving for six months the morning following graduation. It was eating Lamar alive that he hadn't yet told his team that he was going on a joce.

Then, his phone vibrated. It was a group text from Nikki; she had put together a party for Lamar and his class. Live performances from rappers from all over would be in the building. Like Lamar hiding that he had to leave for a while, Nikki still made sure to hide that she was pregnant.

The night of the graduation party, hustlers from around the area came out to show Lamar some love and support. Lamar and Coop were showered with gifts and treated like kings. Once the party was over, Lamar was invited to Nikki's house. Knowing he was about to leave, he took her up on her offer. Nikki intended to make

Lamar forget he wanted Lala or to fly Shanterrica out. As Lamar pulled out a condom, Nikki started to suck his dick. After a few minutes into it, he had nutted. But he didn't know that the damage had already been done. Nikki slapped her wet ass pussy all over Lamar's face, leaving it drenched like a waterfall.

The next morning, Lamar found himself waking up to breakfast in bed as if he had just slept beside his wife. Around half past noon, he finally got out of bed to start the day. This Sunday, Coop would be with his family. Nikki was trying to recover from the last night as she took a cold shower for the longest escapade she had ever encountered. This was a day of rest. So, no work for the entire familia. Lamar decided that although it was too late to make it to church service, he would chill with his mom—especially since she didn't know he would be turning himself in only a few days later.

As Lamar drove to town and pulled into his mother's yard, he could only smile because of the way she was living. Lamar had bought her a 2800 square foot brick house in a subdivision with a brick fence surrounding it. Lamar then walked into his mother's house as she was cooking Sunday dinner. It was like he knew his mother needed to see him. Sitting on a stool at the kitchen island, Lamar watched as Ms. Carroll placed a pan into the oven.

"Ma, I got some bad news, and this is not easy to tell you."

"Go ahead, tell me."

"Well, Mama... I got to go away for a while."

Ms. Carroll looked at Lamar momentarily and said, "I knew the day was coming. I just didn't know how soon."

"It will be the day after graduation... for six months."

Ms. Carroll shouted with rage, screaming Lamar's name. "How could you not tell me when you first found out?"

The only thing Lamar could do was hold his hands above his head and shrug his shoulders. After giving his mother a quick kiss on the cheek, he went into the living room to take a call from Smitty, who said that he was thankful for the opportunity he had been given. Lamar told him, "You family," before hanging up.

He then lay on the couch and waited for dinner.

After Lamar ate, he lay back down and stayed at his mother's for the night. At one point through the night, he rolled over and saw his mother looking at him.

"I wish your father would have been in your life," she said. "Maybe you would have turned out better."

\* \* \*

Graduation day had come, and everyone was excited. The school was packed with damn near half one side in support of Y.I.C. When Lamar and Coop walked across the stage, you would've thought the president had come up to give a speech. The two were well respected and loved.

After the ceremony, they walked out, and Coop's eyes dropped the instant he saw a big red bow wrapped around a brand-new Corvette. He damn near jumped into Lamar's arms, thanking him. Lamar had dropped sixty-four bands on the new Vette for Coop, the one who had been through the most with him. Opening the door to the sports car, Coop found a bag with about ten bands and instructions on what to do next. Lamar was letting Coop know he was about to leave, but he never truly came out with it. Just a note saying, "Until next time, captain."

Nikki walked up to Lamar to hug and kiss him just as Ms. Carroll made a statement that she liked Nikki because she was classy. Then Nikki handed Lamar a gift bag containing an iced-out Rolex she had dropped eleven bands on. She had also put a little something extra in the bag. It was the three pregnancy tests... all showing positive results.

Lamar looked at Nikki as she congratulated him, walking off with all the style and grace she possessed.

# Chapter Six

I t was Wednesday morning, and aside from the positive test results he had seen the night before, Lamar knew he had to turn himself in to begin his six-month sentence. The secretary spoke as he entered Mr. Sveirman's office carrying a duffle bag filled with cash, but Lamar wasn't in the mood for small talk.

When Mr. Sveirman saw him, he asked if he was ready to get this over with. But he could tell by the look on Lamar's face something was wrong. Lamar then dropped the duffle bag on Mr. Sveirman's desk and told him to handle the situation. Lamar took a seat and explained that he couldn't leave now because he had just found out he was about to be a father. Mr. Sveirman told Lamar not to worry, the situation was handled, and congratulations on becoming a father.

As Lamar left the attorney's office, he called Nikki and asked her to meet him at his mom's house.

After hanging up, Lamar called his mother and asked if she was home; he needed her to be a part of an important conversation that would change their lives. As he got off the phone with his mother, he thought of a million ways to get out of the streets because he knew how it felt to grow up without a father.

**\* \* \***

Nikki was grinding as usual but knew she had to go when her boss called. Arriving at Ms. Carroll's house, she decided to go on in. Once she got inside, she complimented Lamar's mother on how amazing her house looked and how neat she kept it.

"What brings you by?"

"Lit Red... I mean Lamar... called and asked me to come over and meet him here."

Ms. Carroll sat in her recliner, wondering what her son was up to.

Nikki asked, "Well... did he mention what he wanted?"

"No. He only asked if I was at home and said I was about to be part of an important conversation."

Lamar had just pulled into the subdivision, and as he was coming around the curb, he could see Nikki's white

Audi already parked in the yard. He then entered his mom's house in a different manner than his mother had ever seen before. Nikki greeted him with a hug and kissed him on the cheek. He walked over to hug and kiss his mom.

"What is all this about?" she asked, sitting back in her recliner.

Lamar turned and looked at Nikki while smiling, showing all his pearly white teeth. "I don't know if you've been praying these past two nights to keep me home, but it worked."

Nikki stopped him and asked, "Where were you planning on going?"

"Well, this morning, I was supposed to turn myself in to the Feds to do six months."

"Who was going to lead the team while you were gone?" Nikki interrupted.

"It doesn't matter now because I'm not going anywhere," he responded, reaching into his pocket and pulling out the pregnancy test he had been given by Nikki the night before and handing it to his mother.

She began to scream and cry tears of joy. "Who is the lucky lady? Who's about to have my grandchild?"

Lamar briefly sighed and then told her Nikki was carrying her grandchild.

Ms. Carroll grabbed Nikki and held her as they cried together. "When did you find out you were pregnant?" she asked.

Nikki looked at Lamar and then at Ms. Carroll before revealing that she had known since their trip to Dallas.

"Was that why you missed out on brunch and were distant from the team that weekend?

With regret and guilt, she responded with a simple "yes."

"Have you told your parents the exciting news yet?" Ms. Carroll asked.

Nikki began crying, explaining that her dad was a pimp and a hustler who had died from AIDS some years ago, and she hadn't seen her mother in eleven years — that she had run off and gotten remarried, leaving Nikki with her grandmother. Ms. Carroll felt sorry for Nikki and asked if she knew how to contact her mom.

"The only person who knows that information is my grandmother."

At that moment, Lamar got a call from Smitty and stepped outside. Smitty told Lamar that he had moved his twenty pounds for the week and needed more. The main reason Lamar was on the boss level is because of the connections he had in the game and with workers like Coop and Smitty, which would keep him there for a very long time. Lamar told Smitty he would have a load delivered in an hour, and then he returned to the house, calling Nikki into the foyer.

"You are no longer a hustler of this organization."

"How can I be dropped from the team after pushing thirty bricks a week?" Lamar paused briefly before saying anything, then told her, "You're pregnant with my child, so whatever you need or desire, I will handle that for you, ma."

"I like my own money, and I've been independent since I was sixteen. I don't need your money."

"Until I recruit someone to take over your area, Coop now has it," he replied. "End of discussion."

Nikki nodded, knowing her boss and baby daddy was serious about the situation. But she had a few other things on her mind that she was not enthusiastic to say in front of Lamar's mother. So, she asked her whether she minded if she and Lamar could have a private conversation.

"If it's to be said," Ms. Carroll replied, "then say it. Because we are family... and that's why we are here."

Nikki took a deep breath and asked Lamar, "How are you supposed to give me what I desire when you're focused on giving yourself to others?"

Lamar looked lost. "What are you talking about?"

"I want more between us than just a boss-and-employee type of relationship, but you're giving Shanter-rica everything I want and desire. You spend time with her, making her feel loved and making love to her, and it should be me. I want that same shit... I'm the one involved with you! So, Lamar... there you have it."

Lamar looked at his mother, speechless, and as she looked back at him, the room suddenly got quiet. Needing to clear his head, he left his mother's house and

called Coop, telling Coop to meet him at the slab asap—
he needed to talk.

Nikki sighed, and as she left out behind Lamar, told
Ms. Carroll she also needed some time to herself. Ms.
Carroll was in disbelief at the conversation. It made her
need a joint and a glass of wine. But first, she walked
Nikki to the car.

* * *

Coop made it to the slab before Lamar since it was just
around the corner from his location. As he patiently
waited for his boss to show up, he could only imagine
what the emergency was about. Lamar drove up slowly
and exited his car with Crown Royal, taking shots
straight from the bottle. Coop instantly knew something
was bothering him.

"Bro, what is the emergency meet-up?" Coop asked.

"You're about to be an uncle," Lamar said, dropping
his head.

Coop was extremely happy and asked, "Man, I knew
you and Shanterrica would eventually have a baby."

Lamar looked at Coop and hit the bottle again,
shaking his head.

"Sooo..." Coop said slowly. "Well, nigga... who is it?"

"Nikki."

"Fuck!"

"Something wrong?" Lamar asked, looking at his friend. "What's the problem, nigga?"

"Man, I wanted the pussy, and you beat me to it."

Lamar just laughed. "You dumb! But seriously, I found out last night after graduation."

Coop went on to tell Lamar he knew he was going to sleep with Nikki before he did because of what Nikki told him. Lamar had the bottle up to his mouth, then pulled it down and asked Coop, "What the fuck are you talking about?"

"Remember the night at 'The Little Den' when we walked out?"

"Yeah," said Lamar.

"Well, I asked her to fuck, but she said 'no' and to ask you how good the pussy was after you hit it."

Lamar could only up the bottle and look at Coop in amazement.

"You talk to Neiko?" Coop asked, trying to change the subject.

Lamar let it slide since he did need to call Neiko to see how business was going. It was mid-week, so he figured Neiko would've moved twenty pounds or more of the Kush by now. However, during the call, Neiko stated that he had only moved seventeen, which upset him. Lamar felt Neiko was playing with his money—the last thing he would let anyone do. "I need you to have twenty pounds moved by Sunday," Lamar said before hanging up and telling Coop he was going home to get some rest. "The past 72 hours have been all up and down."

As Lamar headed home, he spotted a Chevy Tahoe following him. With every turn, Lamar's killer instinct quickly kicked in with his finger on the trigger, ready to fire. Pulling into his driveway, he noticed the Tahoe had stopped and waited for him to get out before slowly driving away.

* * *

Days had passed, and no one heard from Lamar, which was highly unusual. Meanwhile, Nikki had gotten an address from her grandmother on a possible location of her mother. Nikki always wanted to find her mother. But deep down inside, she wondered if it was worth the hassle.

The following Tuesday morning, Nikki showed up at Ms. Carroll's house and asked if she would go to the address with her. Since Ms. Carroll had taken an interest in Nikki, she agreed. But once they pulled up to the address, it was a bank. Nikki then asked Ms. Carroll if she was sure that she had put the correct address in the GPS. Doublechecking, the older woman looked at Nikki and nodded, "Yes." The two then entered the bank, pretending to open an account. They had only been seated momentarily before a woman entered the lobby and directed them to an office. As Nikki looked around, she spotted her mother sitting at the desk.

"May I help you?"

Nikki had not rehearsed what she would say the day she saw her mother again. Seeing her speechless, Ms. Carroll spoke up and said they wanted to open an account.

"Well..." the lady said, without ever looking up from her computer, "You'll need identification and a minimum of $500 to open an account."

"Mother, I have $20K to deposit into a new account."

The lady stopped typing and, seeing Nikki's face, looked like she had seen a ghost. "Nicole Reginae Williams."

Nikki held her head down, crying. "I wanted to find you, so I could let you know you're about to become a grandmother."

Nikki and her mother cried as they hugged each other. They hadn't spoken or seen one another in more than a decade. As her mother told her that she knew everything going on with her, all from her grandmother, Nikki noticed her graduation picture on her mother's desk—and a photo of her walking across the stage.

Coop couldn't take not hearing from his brother-boss. When he went to Lamar's house, he saw that Lamar hadn't checked his mailbox in days. Coop had a key, so he let himself in only to find Lamar in bed with his phone on "Do Not Disturb."

Luckily, Lamar knew the unexpected visitor had to be Coop or his mother, so he left his gun on the dresser. He had been thinking of giving the streets up and going to college when Coop had come over, but it was just a thought. He then told Coop he wasn't ignoring him but needed time alone. So much was going on.

Coop then informed Lamar that someone had broken into the trap house. He knew that Lamar would get up... and he did.

"Give me twenty minutes to shower, and then we will shake the spot."

Coop stepped out ahead of his boss. But as he left, he passed a Chevy Tahoe coming down the street. Within a moment, Lamar also walked out of the house, and as he was locking the door, the exact vehicle that had followed him days before pulled up and opened fire on him.

Coop heard the shots and punched the Corvette to the max, quickly racing back. When he pulled up, he found his brother slumped over in a puddle of blood. Deciding not to wait for an ambulance, Coop put Lamar in the Vette and drove him to the hospital.

# Chapter Seven

M s. Carroll had just told Nikki's mother how close they had gotten when her phone started to vibrate. When she answered, she hit the speaker, and a man spoke. "Ms. Carroll, this is Detective Miller. I am calling to inform you that your son has been shot multiple times." The older woman screamed and dropped the phone.

"Ms. Carroll? Are you there?" the detective asked as the phone went silent. Hanging up, he called again. This time though, Ms. Carroll stayed on the line long enough to question if her son was okay. The detective refused to give any information over the phone. Reluctantly, he provided her with the location of her son.

Ms. Carroll again hung up as Nikki was comforted by her mother while tears flooded her face. Nikki's mom saw that Ms. Carroll's nerves were upset, so she told her boss she had an emergency and needed to leave. Nikki, Ms. Carroll, and her mother all got into Nikki's mother's BMW truck and headed directly toward Shreveport. Ms. Carroll then asked Nicole's mom what her name was.

"My name is Balinda, but everyone calls me Linda."

"I'm sorry we had to meet this way, but I'm so thankful for you taking us over here."

"It's no problem," Linda said to Ms. Carroll, "I'm just happy to see my daughter."

Balinda spotted a Louisiana State Trooper on the highway, clocking the traveler's speed as she passed him. Suddenly his lights came on, but she wasn't letting off the gas for anything. As she continued to drive, her phone suddenly rang. Since it was connected to the radio, the name appeared as well. When she answered, a man's voice came through the speaker.

"Linda, why are you doing 90 mph coming down I-20?"

Balinda knew that the L.S.P., who was out clocking drivers was none other than her loving husband. He then asked her where she was going in such a hurry. She explained to him that Nikki had come to see her to inform her that she was about to be a grandmother. The father's mother had accompanied her, and while they were there, she had received a phone call stating that her son had been shot and was taken to L.S.U. in Shreveport.

After hearing that, Linda's husband said, "I'll give you a call right back."

Nikki couldn't believe what she had just heard... *her stepfather was a cop*. As they continued driving down the highway, Linda asked Nikki about Lamar. But Nikki redirected the conversation. "I just want to get to the hospital to see him."

Linda's phone rang again. Her husband told her to get behind him so that he could escort them to the hospital. As they were coming down the highway, Nikki received a call from Smitty about a rumor going around saying Lamar was dead, but no one was confirming it. She was already in shock and couldn't stay on the phone without crying, so she hung up.

Right then, the car abruptly stopped; cars were lined up miles away from the hospital. Traffic was moving but extremely slow. Anxiety-inducing slow.

When they finally reached the hospital, they saw a crowd outside with lighted candles supporting Lamar. Even though he was young, he had already made a name for himself and was known all over. As Officer Miller pushed his way through the throng to the hospital entrance, people noticed Ms. Carroll on the passenger side of the BMW truck.

Upon entering the hospital, they asked the desk clerk where they could find Lamar Carroll. She checked the computer but couldn't find anyone by that name. Ms. Carroll then pulled out her phone to call Detective Miller, wanting to know where the hell her son was. Detective Miller then came behind the three ladies and told them to follow him as he led the way to the hospital chapel, explaining that he had gotten a call to keep Lamar in a private room with maximum security. Ms. Carroll then asked the detective who called him.

"The chief of y'all's town and a federal agent named Denise Butler," he said.

Nikki wasn't worried about any of that; she only wanted to see Lamar. However, when she asked the detective why they couldn't see him, she was told he was in surgery.

After escorting the trio into the worship room, Detective Miller, who was also a minister, asked if they minded if he prayed for and with them. Just a second before he started to pray, Balinda's husband walked into the room. Detective Miller looked up and saw Officer Miller, and the two immediately started hugging as if it were a family reunion. When they finally broke their hug, they told the ladies that they were brothers who hadn't seen each other in more than fifteen years.

"Do anyone stay in touch anymore?" Ms. Carroll asked as everyone laughed.

The detective then asked them to bow their heads as he began to pray. Immediately after praying, Office Miller received a call and was told to look outside. Both brothers headed for the door. Nikki wanted to know what was wrong, and instead of getting her upset, they only told her it was official police business. By the time the pair had made it down to the hospital's front entrance, the crowd had grown.

"Who is this guy?" Officer Miller asked.

"He's an eighteen-year-old with the mayor and chief of police of four towns on his payroll," his brother responded. "The F.B.I. has been after him, but with his line of money, the cases always vanish into the wind. He has killed at least thirty people we know of, well suspected. But the people are so scared of him that they refuse to testify."

"Sounds like a mafia boss if you ask me."

Detective Miller slowly nodded. "He runs this organization by the name of Y.I.C., and when he says something, they do it."

"Does Nikki know about this guy?" Officer Miller asked.

Looking at his brother as if he were crazy, Detective Miller said, "Nikki is a part of Y.I.C. She works for him!"

Officer Miller started to scratch his head and wondered if his wife knew all this information.

Back upstairs, Ms. Carroll was receiving phone calls left to right like she was running a business. All of Lamar's team had called either Ms. Carroll's phone or Nikki's, except for Coop. It was oddly strange because Nikki called over forty-five times and sent text messages back-to-back, but Coop never returned a call nor replied.

Smitty and Jasmine showed up at the hospital and asked Nikki to come down to meet them, leaving Ms. Carroll and Balinda alone.

"I couldn't imagine being in your shoes at this moment and remaining strong," Linda said. "But I do know how it feels to be worried about your child. I could have come back and gotten Nikki and given her a better life, but I had to find myself. So as a parent, I could only imagine how you feel."

Ms. Carroll thanked her for the cheerful speech, yet she still hadn't heard a word about Lamar.

Nikki got down to the first floor and was surprised to see Neiko. Even though he called, he got with Smitty, and they came together. They were each wearing the t-shirts that Lamar had made for them, which quickly identified them as a team.

Officer Miller saw the group heading upstairs and told Detective Miller to look, who nodded.

"That's Y.I.C.," he said. "But the captain isn't here. I haven't seen him since we left the hospital."

As the group exited the elevator, the doctor came through the double doors asking for the family of Lamar Carroll. Everyone stood around as he spoke and gave an update. Dr. Collins told them Lamar was in critical condition but would make it through.

Ms. Carroll then asked when they could see him. The

doctor said he was heavily sedated and needed to rest before anyone could see him. Nikki could only say, "Thank you, Lord," as she felt relieved knowing her child's father would live. Ms. Carroll then left and walked downstairs as everyone followed her like they were her bodyguards. When she stepped outside, a podium had been set up for her to speak to the media. She started by telling the crowd how thankful she was for everyone coming out to support her son and that he needed to rest as he was still in critical condition.

"Now, if y'all don't mind... at this time, in honor and respect for Lamar, may you all return to your cars and head home so he can rest peacefully," Ms. Carroll said, knowing she had to say something for the people to leave the hospital grounds.

As Ms. Carroll re-entered the building, a woman approached her with a gun on her hip and a badge, asking how Lamar was doing.

"Do I know you, Miss?" Ms. Carroll asked. "And how do you know my son?"

"I'm Denise Butler, ma'am. I'm sorry that we haven't met yet, but I used to spend time with Lamar. And when I heard the news of what happened, I made the call to have him put under maximum security."

Ms. Carroll looked over at Nikki and back at Denise. Then, under her breath said, "My nerves not good for this hoe ass son of mine," as she walked off, telling Denise to follow her.

It was hours before anyone could see Lamar, and when they finally did, he was still unconscious. Ms. Carroll walked into the room and couldn't believe she was looking at her son lying in a hospital bed like he was dead and hopeless. But she kept her faith in God that her son would be okay.

Everyone went in one by one to have their moment alone with Lamar. After Ms. Carroll, Nikki went in with her mother. As she lay her hand on his chest, her cries could be heard down the hallway.

"God, why did this have to happen to him?!"

Her mother knew it was time to get her out of the room at that moment cause stress could cause her to have a miscarriage.

After Nikki left, Neiko and Smitty went in to show their respect, but Smitty only stayed in the room for a few minutes. Denise was the last to go in. While shutting the door, Ms. Carroll stuck her foot in to eavesdrop through the crack.

"Lamar Carroll, I know you'll tell me crybabies don't get no love," she said, tears rolling down her face. "But Baby, you done ran the streets and earned your crown. How am I supposed to go home and tell your three-year-old daughter that her father will never see her again? Please, Lamar... leave the streets alone." Denise then sighed hard as she tried to catch her breath. Before walking out, she said a quiet prayer.

Ms. Carroll pretended to be leaving the restroom when she came out. Just then, Denise received a phone call, and she told whoever it was to come upstairs to the sixth floor and make sure they had all they needed. She returned to the waiting area and asked Ms. Carroll to walk with her. As they started to walk, Ms. Carroll could only think of what she had heard moments ago. Three men approached them and asked Denise what they needed to do.

"Your client is Lamar Carroll," Denise said. "He's in maximum security. Two of you are to sit at the door, and one is to stay in the room."

Ms. Carroll told Denise, "Thank you for all you're doing for my son. I'm sure he'll be thankful too." She then pulled out her cell to call Coop again, but it went straight to voicemail.

Nikki had stepped outside to meet her stepfather and to talk to her mother. Balinda asked about her and Lamar. But just before she could share, Officer Miller reached out to hug her and said, "You must be Nicole." Since it was his first time meeting her, he wanted to ensure she was comfortable around him; therefore, he took Balinda and Nikki out to eat. The restaurant was down the road, so they all got into his patrol unit.

After being seated, Nikki told her mother she was a hustler on Lamar's team, the only female hustler he had. Balinda thought Lamar was a pimp, so she told Nikki her body was too precious to be sold.

"Lamar isn't a pimp. He's one of the most powerful people around."

"Hmph... where did that twenty thousand dollars come from that you came to deposit in the bank?"

"I run the town I'm in. When it comes to drugs, I'm good at it... the $20K was from the $170K I made last week."

Balinda and Officer Miller both looked very surprised. Balinda was stunned to learn that her child was into drugs, let alone selling them.

* * *

After everyone left the hospital to eat or head home, Ms. Carroll sat in the waiting room, grateful knowing her son would live to see another day.

Nevertheless, deep down inside, she knew it was far from over.

# Chapter Eight

"Why am I here? What's going on?"

Those were the first words from Lamar's mouth as he awoke. He had been out for so long that he didn't remember a thing that had taken place. Nikki rushed to his bedside, comforting Lamar and letting him know that everything was going to be okay. She then explained to him that he had been shot and was just waking up from surgery. Lamar asked her how he got to the hospital.

"Coop drove you to the hospital," Nikki said. But we haven't been able to reach him. That was over twenty-seven hours ago."

Lamar looked around the room filled with flowers, cards, and balloons and said to himself, "Damn, somebody must love me," cracking a smile.

The guard got out of his chair and said, "Mr. Carroll,

I'm glad you're okay. I will call my boss and let her know that you're up and talking."

"Who the fuck is you?" Lamar asked.

"I'm special agent Tyler," the guard answered, and my boss is Denise Butler."

Lamar could only glance at Nikki before telling her that there was something she needed to know. But Ms. Carroll walked into the room with someone she needed to discuss with him. Ms. Carroll would take care of Lamar's bills every month, never noticing the $2500 he would deposit into a personal account every month. Little did she know it was Denise Butler's account.

Looking at Nikki, she told her to close her ears. "Lamar Deon Carroll, don't you ever scare me like that no damn more."

Lamar laughed and said, "Quit playing like you was scared, Mama. You know I'm built Ford tough," before showing off his bright whites and looking around for his phone. Luckily his mother had gone to his house and noticed it under his car tire.

She reached into her purse and gave it to him, saying, "The president's phone is probably not that damn busy."

Suddenly, there was a knock at the door. Ms. Carroll said, "Come on in." Lamar was hoping like hell it wasn't another female. Thankfully, it was Dr. Collins. Ms. Carroll thanked Dr. Collins for saving her son's life with a massive hug.

Dr. Collins looked at Lamar and said, "Whoever shot you wanted you dead, son. You're lucky to be alive."

"Sir, I owe you my life, and I will repay you as soon as I get out of this hospital."

"You don't owe me anything; you owe my wife. See, my father-in-law's funeral was going on when I got the call to come in. In order to save you, I had to leave her. So, from one Black man to another, you can repay me by turning your life around and making a change," the doctor said before telling him to get well and walking out of the room.

Lamar looked at Nikki and said, "I need my MacBook."

But Nikki hadn't driven and didn't have her car. So, Lamar asked his mother to find the nearest Best Buy to get him a new one... no matter the price. Ms. Carroll knew he needed time alone because he had just gotten his phone back. So, she asked Nikki to ride with her.

After the two left the room, Lamar knew he had to call Denise to talk to her. But after trying her phone, it went straight to voicemail. Lamar then called each of his team members to let them know he was up and talking, but he couldn't get in touch with his captain after repeatedly trying Coop's phone. A knock on the door interrupted him, and the special agent peeped in and asked if he wanted company. Lamar told him to let whoever it was in for now.

It was LaLa.

"LaLa, how did you find out where I was... and do you know what happened to me?"

"Have you seen the news lately?"

Shaking his head, she handed him her phone to show him a video of the news clip aired two days earlier.

A known mob boss fatally shot multiple times while coming out of his home is in critical condition. Rumors are he has passed, but we will keep you updated.

"Man, these people really thought I was dead," Lamar exclaimed as LaLa swiped to another video.

Thousands have gathered to show their respect around the hospital with candles for the known mob boss Lamar Deon Carroll. As police try to control the crowd, more people show up as we speak.

LaLa said, "I could only imagine how your mother felt after seeing this, Lamar. Do you ever stop to think how she will feel to lose her only child at an early age to the streets?"

Lamar lay back in the hospital bed. "It's easy getting in the streets, but it's hard getting out once you have been living that life for so long."

LaLa didn't seem to understand, so before she left, she kissed Lamar and told him, "I have always wanted you, but since I stay under my parent's roof, I have to respect their decision."

As LaLa left the room, Lamar told her to stay in touch if she needed anything. LaLa smiled and continued to walk out the door. Even though she had made Lamar's day, he was still worried about Coop because he hadn't yet answered any calls or texts. If anyone could get Coop to answer the phone, it was Diamond. So, Lamar knew he had to call her. After calling Diamond, Lamar put his phone on mute to see what was happening with his brother as Diamond called Coop on three-way.

Coop answered the phone, and you could tell he was down from the sound of his voice. Diamond knew she had to put her sexy voice on for Coop. The two were like night and day—they had a weird relationship. Diamond proceeded to ask Coop what the problem was, knowing from the tone of his voice that something was bothering him. Coop then opened up to let her have it.

"I feel bad for what happened to Lamar. If only I wouldn't have left when he told me to, I could've..."

"You could've got shot also, Coop," she said, stopping him.

He knew she was right, but he felt guilty about the situation. "It was a Chevy Tahoe meeting me as I was leaving... and when I was headed back to Lamar's house, that same Tahoe passed me speeding."

At that moment, Lamar remembered there had been a Tahoe following him a few days before he got shot. So, he texted Diamond and told her to tell Coop that he wanted to see him. Still on three-way, Diamond told Coop that Lamar wanted to see him, but Coop insisted he wasn't ready to see his brother in a hospital bed.

Just then, Ms. Carroll and Nikki returned to the hospital with the new MacBook. She couldn't understand why her son needed a laptop at that moment, but he did. When he finished setting up everything, he could log into his security cameras and replay the day everything happened. After reviewing the video, he caught a license plate on the truck. He told Nikki he needed her to go home and handle something, insisting that his mother also go home to rest because he was okay. But this was only a cover-up to hide his thoughts.

After the two women had left the room for the second time, Lamar sent a text to Denise to give her the plate information to see what she could find out. The nurse had also come to give him his pain meds which would have him out for a while.

Lamar woke up punching in a rage after having a dream about what had happened. He knew it would be only a matter of time before he found out who it was, but he had to wait on the information to get back to him. He tried hard to go back to sleep but could only watch the video over and over again. With a sore body, Lamar knew he couldn't rest, and the video constantly made him mad.

He decided to start shopping for Mother's Day, knowing it was the next day and he couldn't leave. Ms.

Carroll had everything a person could possibly want, so buying her a gift would be challenging. Knowing his mother loved to wear necklaces, he needed to find her one with sentimental meaning.

So, Lamar called up his jeweler, who had made his pendants, to get one containing pink diamonds.

Johnny Dang had heard the news about his friend and told him the necklace was on him. Only a few hours away, he personally promised to drive the pendant down to show his respect.

The day was going by fast, and Lamar still hadn't made his way back to sleep. Knowing that he needed it, he finally forced himself to rest. He woke up the following day to a happy voice screaming "Daddy" as she was super excited to see him. Denise had brought their daughter to see him since she knew that would cheer him up.

"Aaliyah! "Lamar yelled as he reached his arms out for her while smiling.

As Lamar and Aaliyah bonded, Denise dismissed Special Agent Tyler and told him to give them some time alone. While playing with his daughter, Lamar told Denise to check her phone, putting his down. He had deposited $5K into her account for Mother's Day. Denise didn't need Lamar's money and didn't want it, but she knew it wasn't a no in the scenario.

"Can we have a serious conversation?" she asked.

Knowing that when Denise said something like that,

she meant business, Lamar gave Aaliyah his phone so that he could focus on what Denise wanted to discuss.

"I'm not going to sit here and lie as if I don't care or still have feelings for you," Denise said, "but I will refuse to put my child in any harm's way by being with you, Lamar. We have a three-year-old together, and your life scares me. What if you had been shot elsewhere and wouldn't have made it to the hospital? Do you even think of it? Like, Lamar... come on, something has to give! You were fifteen when we had Aaliyah; you have so much power over things—your mother didn't even have to sign her birth certificate after you. I have people at my job blowing me up, asking was Aaliyah's father a mob boss and killer."

When Denise finally took a breath, she started shedding tears before continuing. "The life you live may be good for you, but you are living and hurting the ones that love you."

Lamar was quiet for so long after Denise finished talking she had to ask him if he had anything to say. He looked at Aaliyah and said, "This was one of my greatest creations; she had been my motivation since you had her. I was busy hustling for me and her future. If I made $100,000, I would put back $50,000 for her. Denise, look at me. I just graduated high school and have a child. When it comes to being with you, don't get me wrong, I want to be... but look at how it would affect your career. You have something good going for you, and I wouldn't want to be in your way if I was to get with you."

Denise had wanted to know if there was any change in him so they could work on a relationship. She got everything except that.

Ms. Carroll was headed toward Lamar's room when she saw Special Agent Tyler sitting in the hallway. "Aren't you supposed to be inside the room?" The agent told her that Lamar was having a special visit, and he had been told to step out.

"How long have they been in there?"

"Oh, about thirty to forty-five minutes."

When Ms. Carroll opened the door, she saw a little girl who looked exactly like her son and the lady that had her son put into maximum security. Lamar had been hiding Aaliyah from his mother, but he didn't know that she already knew Aaliyah was her grandchild. When she walked into the room, Lamar and Denise looked at each other as they were saying, *what the fuck are we going to do or say?*

"Mama, happy Mother's Day," Lamar said before telling Denise to hand her the bag off the table.

Ms. Carroll sat on the edge of the bed and opened it as she saw the pendant saying Y.I.C. with pink diamonds. She smiled and told Lamar, "Thank you," but then said, "Well, I guess I got two good gifts today—I got a beautiful necklace and a chance to meet my granddaughter."

Lamar asked her how she knew that was his daughter

and when did she find out. She told him she heard Denise when he was unconscious days before, asking how she could go home and tell their daughter that her father was not coming home. Denise looked at Ms. Carroll and told Lamar she didn't know she heard her. Lamar looked at Aaliyah and asked her who that was, and when Aaliyah responded, "That's granny," you couldn't tell who was crying the most, Ms. Carroll or Denise. Lamar told his mother, "It's about time we come together and let all our secrets out."

"You're right, son," Ms. Carroll replied, calling someone and giving them Lamar's room number.

When Lamar asked who she had called, she only said the person would be there within a few minutes. In the meantime, Ms. Carroll played with Aaliyah, telling her how much she was going to spoil her. Soon, someone knocked on the door, and a tall man entered.

"Aren't you Mr. Craft, the owner of Craft Funeral Homes?" Denise asked.

The gentleman nodded.

"Why would you call him?" Lamar asked his mother. "I'm not dead."

Ms. Carroll turned and looked at her son. "Because he's your father."

# Chapter Nine

Shocked by the news he had just heard, Lamar asked for everyone to leave the room except Mr. Craft. Aaliyah was a daddy's baby, so she cried for Lamar when Denise grabbed her to exit the room. Lamar looked at Mr. Craft and asked, "If you're my father, where have you been?"

"I have tried time after time to be in your life. Your mother told me you had a good life without me, then changed her number."

Lamar reflected on the night of his graduation, looking at Mr. Craft. "You were at my graduation in the back corner with two women and another man. You all were dressed alike."

Mr. Craft nodded. "I was with your two sisters and brother. I've built an empire for all my kids, and being that your mother kept you away, it hurt me that you never got a chance to be a part of it," he said, moving toward the door.

Before he could leave, Lamar said, "I'll get your number from my mother and give you a call, okay? Oh, and you can tell my mother to head home also."

\* \* \*

Later, after the nurse had given Lamar his pain medicine, which instantly put him to sleep, when he woke up, he heard a voice saying, "If you're dead, you can't provide. But if you hustle, you won't struggle." He immediately knew it was Coop, and as he looked over to his left, he first saw Special Agent Tyler sitting in the chair, keeping watch. But standing next to him was Coop. Lamar was happy as hell to see his brother.

"Motherfucker, you got blood all over my damn Corvette trying to save you," Coop teased, leaning over and hugging Lamar.

"Take your ass to the lot and buy another one on me," Lamar replied, laughing." What took him so long to come to see me?" he asked, suddenly serious. He already knew the answer but still wanted to hear it from Coop himself.

"Man, it hurt my soul when I had to take you to the hospital, not knowing if you were going to make it or not. Plus, I just couldn't see you like this." Lamar could understand where Coop was coming from. Lamar then asked Coop if he had been grinding or what he had been doing.

"Man, you know I been grinding. But bro, you'll never believe who I done fucked."

"Who?"

"Lisa Davis... our classmate Katrina's mama."

"You a got damn lie!" Lamar exclaimed. "That fucking woman married, and I don't believe she'll be the type to cheat or fuck around."

Coop pulled out his phone and showed Lamar the messages before he heard Lamar say, "Damn, I should've shot my shot."

Coop said, "Man, she came to me after hearing what happened to you and said I want to take your mind off everything. She grabbed my phone and texted her number, telling me to stay tuned."

"Nigga, finish the damn story, ole trifling ass nigga."

"On everything," Coop continued. "I was at home around 10:45 and heard my phone go off... it was her.

The text said:

*Best Western Room 359*
*Get here. There's a key in the driver side door of my car*
*Lock the car doors when you get the key*

"I tried calling her to see if it was meant for me, but the phone went straight to voicemail."

"Man, you got to be the dumbest motherfucker to

even think twice about that," Lamar said as the two laughed.

"You would've thought I was a Nascar driver the way I was speeding through town, bro," Coop said.

Even Agent Tyler couldn't help but chuckle this time.

Once the laughter died down, Coop went back to his story. "I got to the motel and saw her car. I made the block and checked the scene before I decided to park. I got out, put my gun in my pants, walked to her car, and started toward the room. I forgot I didn't have but one rubber in the car. So, I told myself maybe it was God's plan like Drake said."

"Man, son... you deserve a first check, but come on, finish it up."

"As I'm approaching the door, my hands are sweating bullets. I stopped and thought *I'm too playa for this shit.* I walked into the room, and it was pitch black and dark. She started spelling my name out... I said to myself *this bitch crazy.* As I got closer to the bed, she turned the light on and put an arch in her back like a damn giraffe."

Special Agent Tyler asked Coop if she was ready to do more. Coop looked at Lamar and said she continued to say, "I heard you like getting your dick sucked, so lay your ass down."

"Talk and quit stopping," Lamar said. "Nigga, this shit is getting good now."

"Bro, when I tell you Mrs. Lisa's mouth so damn offi-cial, boy... I thought she came from the WNBA calling a game. I pushed her back off me. After I busted in her mouth, the freaky bitch looked at me and said, 'get it right.' She lay down in the bed spreading them pink pussy lips of hers and told a nigga to fuck her."

"You a lucky son of a bitch," Lamar said, "but the only reason you got it is because I got shot."

Special Agent Tyler asked Coop and Lamar if they were part of N.W.A.

"No," Lamar answered. "Why?"

"Y'all some ruthless ass lil niggas, but I got mad respect for y'all."

Coop's phone started ringing. He told Lamar, "I done spoke this woman up." Answering it, he put it on speaker.

The females voice on the other end asked Coop what he was doing later that night. Before he could say anything, she told him it had better be her. Coop told her he was busy checking on Lamar and would give her a callback. After getting off the phone, Coop told Lamar, "Enough about me... what's up with you? I see you got the C.I.A. and F.B.I. in here protecting your ass."

Lamar sighed. "Man, this all Denise doing. She had me put in maximum security."

Coop just shook his head. He knew about Denise and Aaliyah but never told Ms. Carroll about them.

Lamar said, "You wouldn't believe who my mama called, sitting right here on this damn hospital bed."

Coop had to joke around with Lamar. He said,

"Probably Barack Obama! Hell, you know you plugged in with everybody."

Lamar laughed and, stopping suddenly, said, "Naw, man, my fucking daddy."

Coop couldn't believe the words that had just come from Lamar's mouth. They had both been told that Lamar's daddy was dead long ago. Lamar told Coop that wasn't all of it, by far.

"You know he was at graduation with two of my sisters and my brother? He owns two funeral homes and sent all his kids to mortician school," Lamar said. Then, knowing that it would only be a matter of time before he dozed off due to the medicine he was on, he warned Coop.

Coop told Lamar to go to sleep; he was gone. But before leaving, he asked him to bow his head so they could pray. Lamar had never heard Coop pray, so it was shocking news to his ears when he said it.

After Coop finished praying, Lamar told him, "Mrs. Lisa got some powerful pussy, because it got you praying, my brother."

All three men in the room laughed.

Coop told his boss, "I'll see you later," and let Lamar drift back to sleep.

* * *

The next morning, as Dr. Collins made his rounds, he spotted his wife coming down the hallway with a bag in her hand. Approaching her, he asked her the reason for the visit and the broad smile on her face.

"I brought my wonderful husband lunch," she said, kissing him. "Especially since you just had that beautiful new vehicle delivered to our house."

Dr. Collins thought his wife was losing it for a second. "What are you talking about?" he asked.

She stepped back and said, "If you didn't buy it, who did?"

The look on the doctor's face was complete bewilderment. She handed him a note that had arrived with the car: Thank you for caring during a time of need when you were in need."

After reading the note, Dr. Collins began laughing, and now Mrs. Collins was the one with a puzzled look on her face... Dr. Collins told his wife to follow him. When the couple walked into Lamar's room, they saw him sitting up and eating breakfast. Dr. Collins introduced his wife and asked if he minded having some company for a second.

Lamar had done his research on Mrs. Collins earlier in the week, but he insisted that she take a seat along with Dr. Collins.

"This morning, a vehicle was delivered with a note to my house..." Dr. Collins started.

Before he could finish his sentence, Nikki walked into

the room. After Lamar made introductions, Dr. Collins continued his inquiry.

"How did you get our address… and why did you buy us a car?" he asked once Lamar confirmed his suspicion.

Lamar sat up in the bed. "They didn't label me as a mob boss for nothing. But I found out your wife's father was a retired veteran, and when you told me the story, I had to do something. I would have written a check, but that was just money, and you already have that. So, I decided to buy a Porsche, painting it camo with your wife's favorite color, dark yellow."

Mrs. Collins was speechless and couldn't believe Lamar had gone out of his way to show his appreciation in such a grand way.

Dr. Collins told Lamar, "Son, you didn't have to do that."

"You didn't have to leave your wife's side and save my life."

Shaking his hand, Dr. Collins told Lamar he had to return to work. As the couple headed towards the door, Nikki gave Mrs. Collins a bag. It was too heavy for her, so she gave it to her husband.

Lamar told Dr. Collins, "I know you go on vacation in three weeks. I have gotten you an all-around trip to Greece to enjoy yourselves."

"I would take you up on that offer, but my priority is sending my daughter to college," Dr. Collins replied.

Lamar told Dr. Collins to open the bag. When he opened it, the couple's mouths dropped. Lamar said, "That's $100K you're looking at. Go enjoy yourself, Doc."

The Collins left the room, and Nikki let Lamar have it—talking so much Lamar had to tell her to stop so he could figure out what she was trying to say. Nikki was explaining to Lamar that she wanted a real relationship with him, and he needed to decide what he wanted to do.

Lamar knew she was serious by the look on her face. He started to quote a rapper named N.B.A. YoungBoy, telling Nikki, "I need you to be there for me. I'm so deep up in the streets. I know niggas want to kill me. That is why I stay clutching on my heat."

At that point, Nikki knew that she was going to be with Lamar.

# Chapter Ten

A few months had passed, and Lamar was back in the streets, hard and heavy, stacking his paper and not taking any shit. The streets were hot, and so was he. People were scared because they couldn't figure out his next move.

Coop was hard out covering his spots and Nikki's at the same time; he never slacked when it came down to making his money. Neiko had gotten with the program. He quickly learned that Lamar wasn't anything to play with after he got word about the smoker Lamar burned. Nikki was approaching the fifth month of her pregnancy, growing like a diamond. Smitty was moving so well that Lamar doubled his weekly weight.

Everything was going well for Y.I.C. until one day, Denise called Lamar and gave him the information from the license plate of the Tahoe that had gunned him down. Lamar answered the phone and, as he got the details, started loading his gun. Denise found out that the truck was a rental from Enterprise with a Cali tag— rented for two weeks to William Tank Smith and returned three days after Lamar had been shot.

Smitty!

Never ready to play too quickly into the hands of others, Lamar decided he would wait some time to get Smitty the way he wanted to. Angry because someone he considered family tried to kill him, and knowing that he needed to calm down, Lamar called Nikki to see what she was up to so they could link up for lunch, but she wasn't answering.

Nikki had gone to the bank, where her mother worked, to finish opening an account. Since her mother knew she was a hustler, she advised her to deposit about $50K.

Balinda was happy to see her daughter and told her coworkers the exciting news of her expecting grandchild. Nikki was so bossed up she had her money transferred from one account to the next. Balinda's supervisor was sitting in the room while the processing was taking place. When Balinda asked Nikki how much she wanted to transfer into the account, she told her 1.3 million, and Balinda and her supervisor started laughing.

Nikki asked when she missed the joke. Balinda was puzzled by the number her daughter had just given her.

The supervisor decided to step out of the room and let the two women have a conversation alone.

"What kind of hustler are you really, Nikki? That's a lot of money to have for one person."

"I never was the type to sleep around with men for money. That's not my M.O.," Nikki responded. "I never been the type to wait on a man to tell me he was gon' do something for me and didn't. I got into pushing drugs, and that became my hustle. Lamar came along and put me into his team... had me making ten times what I was making a week. So basically, I started working for him."

"Well, then... how did you become pregnant by Lamar if you worked for him?"

"Sometimes you fall in love with someone, and that person is a blessing." Nodding her head, Balinda completed the paperwork as Nikki provided her with links to the other two accounts. To her surprise, there was a total of 8.7 million combined in all three accounts.

**\* \* \***

Lamar was so smart about how he moved that he called his father and asked him to meet for lunch in the next hour. Since Mr. Craft wanted to get to know his son, it wasn't a problem. Lamar was still in a rage and still needed to calm down. So, once he got into the car, he fired up a blunt before making his way toward the meeting—leaving everything in the hands of Coop.

Coop had been doing his own detective work by having the stop light cameras in town checked to see if they captured who was in the Tahoe or even the license plate. As Lamar was headed to the meeting, he was thinking of ways he could get back at Smitty; they labeled him a mob boss, so he was prepared to go to work.

Mr. Craft had gotten to the restaurant first and decided to go on in. His assistant and daughter accompanied him. When Lamar arrived, you would've thought the president was rolling in the way they pampered him with wine and walked him to the table, where he was greeted by his father, his half-sister Latonya, and his father's assistant, Chelsea. Mr. Craft was so in disbelief they were having a "sit down" with each other that he was overwhelmed and couldn't start a conversation. Latonya began it for him by telling Lamar it was a pleasure to meet him finally.

"No, it's a pleasure to meet you," Lamar said. "Being that you're my older sister, we should get close to one another."

Mr. Craft told the two that would be a great idea, then offered Lamar an opportunity in the family business. Lamar denied the offer from his father. "It's something you should know about me. I'm my own boss."

Mr. Craft didn't quite understand, so he asked Lamar to elaborate.

"You see, I was labeled a *mob* boss. But I'm just a

boss. I have a crew of four, and they are all good hustlers. The same streets people run and drive on are really mines."

Chelsea knew a street nigga when she saw one, and she couldn't help but have hot flashes when she looked at Lamar's pearly, white-teethed smile. Lamar insisted everyone order what they wanted off the menu because lunch was on him. Latonya wanted to know why Lamar never came around, so when she asked, he told her it wasn't his fault; it was his mother's. For the longest time, Lamar had been told his father was dead.

As the waiter was taking their order, Lamar asked for the best red wine they had, but his father knew he wasn't old enough to purchase it. After the waiter left the table, Mr. Craft asked Lamar if he could ask him some personal questions. Lamar was down to earth, so he didn't mind at all.

"Do you always get your way... and what made you choose the street life?"

Just as Lamar began to answer the first question, Chelsea got up and went to the restroom. Lamar thought to himself *that bitch is weird*. While in the bathroom, Chelsea called her friend, telling her she was having dinner with the mob leader and how fine he was. She then pulled a vibration bullet that was compatible with her phone and stuck it in her pussy before she exited the bathroom. As she sat back down at the table, Lamar was finishing his answer to the second question, and food was being delivered, but she couldn't keep her eyes off him.

While the plates were being placed in front of each of them, Mr. Craft then asked for the purpose of the meeting.

"How much does a funeral usually cost?"

Latonya spoke up. "For a good service, we usually charge around 6k, which includes two limos."

Lamar took a bite of his steak and asked his father how business was going for him. Mr. Craft told him he couldn't complain; he stays busy year-round. Lamar put his fork down and pulled out forty $100 bills kept together by a rubber band, slid it to his father, and told him, "In the next few months, you will have five bodies sent to you. No need for change."

As Lamar smiled and returned to eating his lunch, Mr. Craft realized that his son had no fear in his heart... and Chelsea had orgasms back-to-back.

* * *

After leaving the bank, Nikki went to her doctor's appointment. She was going to have an ultrasound and find out what she was having.

Walking into the clinic, she started to get in her feelings because Lamar was late. As she checked in, she looked around and saw husband and wife together— happy couples. While waiting patiently to see Dr.

Lukewiski, she admired the happy couples' relationships.

Back at the restaurant, Lamar glanced at his watch. Noticing that he would have to leave right away if he were to get to Nikki, he quickly ended the lunch, only telling those at the table that he was running late for an important appointment.

Once Lamar made it to the Women's Clinic, he saw Nikki's car in the parking lot. Then, he spotted her as soon as he walked in... head down, scrolling through her phone. When he sat beside her, Nikki had the biggest smile anyone could've imagined knowing Lamar was taking her pregnancy seriously.

"I never thought you'd make my doctor's appointment; you don't know how much this means to me."

"I'm glad I'm the one to make you happy," Lamar replied before kissing her.

"What made you show up?"

"I been thinking about what you said... and I will love to wake up to you every morning and go to sleep by you every night."

Nikki's smile was so large at that moment that you would've thought Lamar asked her to marry her. The nurse called her to the back and, once the pair were in the examination room, told her to get undressed and that the doctor would be in shortly.

After a short while, Dr. Lukewiski came into the room. Upon seeing Lamar, he stated that he had seen him on T.V. It was nice to meet him. He then asked Nikki if she was ready to see what she was having. Before she could respond, Lamar answered, "Yes," which made the two laugh.

"Looks like we're expecting a baby boy," the doctor announced within a few minutes of peering at the screen in front of them. "Congratulations to both of you!"

"Lamar Deon Carroll Jr.," Lamar said as Nikki agreed and smiled.

As Nikki dressed, following the exam, Lamar's phone rang. Coop had vital information and needed to meet with Lamar… and it couldn't wait.

Lamar told Coop to meet up at the spot in precisely two hours to discuss the problem.

# Chapter Eleven

Breaking news coming up on MTDR Channel 8:

A body, fatally shot multiple times, has been found outside a mother's home. Police said the victim was already dead when they arrived on the scene. Police are asking if anyone has any information about the murder, please contact the Richlend Parish Sheriff's Office.

As Ms. Carroll watched the news, she felt her heart skip a beat from a recent conversation with her son. Lamar had told his mother that bodies would drop one by one for the next month since he had decided to take out the whole crew. So, she knew he was out for revenge.

* * *

Hours earlier, Lamar had met with Coop, who confirmed that Smitty's crew had been in the Tahoe. Lamar figured it had been Smitty's hustlers because Smitty wasn't built like that.

When Smitty received word about his number one hustler, Devin, he rushed to the scene in disbelief. And, because Smitty worked for Lamar, he knew he had to call and tell him what had happened.

"Man, I already know... I'm at the scene now," Lamar said, pulling up and parking alongside Nikki and Neiko. Seeing Devin's mother, he told Smitty to keep his ears open and disconnected the call. Walking over to her, he gave his condolences. "Ma'am, I'm sorry for your loss. Your son was a good man, so I took it upon myself to call Craft Funeral Home, which I'm part owner of, and the funeral expense will be on me."

Devin's mother couldn't believe what she had just heard... someone was willing to pay for her son's funeral.

Before Lamar returned to his car, he grabbed Nikki and told her, "You're five months pregnant. I told you that you're out of the game, meaning you're completely done; you should be out shopping for baby clothes and other baby stuff."

Nikki told Lamar that she only wanted to pay her respects to Devin's mother, but he wasn't trying to hear that. Lamar returned to his car and called his father, telling him he had a body to pick up at 118 Learn Street in Rayville, La. Before hanging up, he said, "One down, four to go."

After Mr. Craft got off the phone with Lamar, he made a call to Ms. Carroll and asked her what exactly was it that Lamar had done.

Ms. Carroll sighed for a second. "Your son is the most feared gangster around and has been that for years. He moves swiftly and has both the mayor and police on payroll. That's who your son is."

Mr. Craft couldn't believe his son was a killer and mob boss. Forty-five minutes later, after Mr. Craft arrived at the murder scene and looked at Devin's body, he couldn't believe how many bullet holes were put into the young man's body. Devin's mother cried so loudly watching her son being bagged that she fainted. Mr. Craft then texted Lamar that he wanted to meet the next day for lunch.

Lamar simply responded, "ok."

The next morning, Ms. Carroll and Nikki went shopping for the baby. Lamar sent Nikki a text saying, "I want to fuck, be at my house by 3." Nikki smiled and told Ms. Carroll, "Your son is something else."

"Yes, he is," Ms. Carroll replied.

While sitting in his office, Mr. Craft thought long and

hard about how he could convince his son to leave the streets and be a part of the funeral home business. He then called Chelsea into the office, asking her to set up reservations at a local steak house for his lunch meeting with Lamar and to get a cashier's check for $2.5 million.

Latonya had stepped into the office while her father instructed Chelsea on what to do and what was happening. Earlier, Mr. Craft had told her to count the bullet holes in Devin's body. "It's a total of fourteen," she said.

Mr. Craft sighed and told her, "I know... it's the work of your brother."

Latonya couldn't believe that her brother had done such a thing. She asked her father how he knew Lamar did it.

"Remember at lunch the other day when he gave us $40k for five funerals and said to keep the change?"

Latonya nodded yes.

"Well... when he called me to pick up this young man, he told me that was one. Four more to go."

LaTonya noticed the worry crossing her father's face. She had never seen him worry about anything before.

Meanwhile, Lamar wondered why his father wanted to meet when they could have spoken over the phone. Coop had come over to Lamar's house. But, since Lamar's blood was still all over Coop's car, Lamar told him to have someone drop him off. Before heading out to meet with his father, he took Coop to pick out a brand-new one.

Lamar noticed that once the pair had hit the interstate, a state trooper slid in behind him, but he wasn't worried.

As they pulled up to the car lot, Coop spotted a Corvette being unloaded from a flatbed and told Lamar that was the one. Lamar didn't care about the price; he owed his life to his friend, so they walked in and told the salesman they wanted that car. The salesman asked Lamar how much he wanted to put down, but Lamar told him never to disrespect him; he buys shit and doesn't pay notes.

The salesman got nervous and started to do the paperwork. Lamar had checked the time and told Coop to walk to his car, where he gave him the duffel bag. He told him he had a meeting and would catch up with him later.

Latonya had just made it back to her office when her phone rang. To her surprise, it was a friend from college.

Sheila told Latonya she had a confession that she needed to get off her chest, which had to be done in person. So, Latonya invited Sheila to come by the office where she was.

Mr. Craft had just received the check from Chelsea and was heading towards the door when he told Brandon that Devin's mother and family would be in around 2 pm to make funeral arrangements.

Not much later, Latonya was sitting at her desk when Sheila arrived at the office to see her. Sheila and Latonya were college friends. They both attended mortician school and finished at the same time. After Latonya invited Sheila to have a seat, she asked what was so important that she couldn't tell her over the phone.

Sheila looked at Latonya and asked, "Did you remember in school I had a thing for this young thug ass dude, but he was too young to be in public with?"

"Yes…"

"Well, I ended up pregnant. Me and the guy separated after Miyleriah was born, and we never spoke again… But every Christmas, I receive a check for $250K from someone out there named Coop."

Latonya said, "Oh, Sheila… you could've told me that over the phone, girl."

But Sheila wasn't done yet. "It's a sign I'm throwing you, girl. Catch it."

Latonya sat back in her chair. "I'm listening," she said, paying close attention.

"Last time we spoke, you told me your brother Lamar Carroll had been shot."

"Yeah, but what he have to do with this?"

Sheila asked Latonya if she had a picture of him. Latonya stepped out to grab a photo from her father's office and returned to show it to Sheila.

"Yeah, that's him," Sheila said. "Lamar Deon Carroll."

"How do you know my little brother?"

"I know him 'cause that's Miyleriah's father."

"What?!"

"Yeah… text him. He'll confirm it."

Seconds later, Lamar's phone vibrated. When he opened it, he saw a picture of Sheila with the message:

*you know her?*

Trying to figure out how Latonya knew Sheila, Lamar figured it didn't matter. So, he sent a text back:

*I know her. That's Miyleriah's mother*

When Latonya received his response, she reached into the side bottom drawer of her desk, pulled out a bottle of wine and two clear glasses to pour up, and said, "Well, I be damn!"

* * *

Lamar had arrived at the restaurant and gotten seated, waiting for his father to arrive. It wasn't long before he saw his father walking into the restaurant's doors, and the two of them were seated together. Seeing a waitress pass by, Lamar told her they were ready to order. While they waited for their food to arrive, Lamar asked his father what the reason for the meeting was. Mr. Craft looked at Lamar and asked whether he cared if he lived or died.

Lamar didn't quite understand where Mr. Craft was coming from, so he asked him what he meant.

Mr. Craft slid Lamar the cashier's check and asked his son if that was enough for him to leave the streets alone. The waitress had just come back with their food before he had a chance to respond; he also had a chance to think.

Lamar started to eat his food and told his father, "With all due respect, I make 2.5 million in a month, and I have something to finish up before I leave the streets alone."

Mr. Craft decided to table the conversation for another time.

Nikki and Ms. Carroll had been out spending money left and right without limit. But Nikki had Lamar's dick going in and out of her on her mind. So, she had decided to go into the dressing room, take a picture of her moist pussy, and send it to him. She knew the nigga she was in love with wanted nothing but the best.

Once the two women finished shopping, Nikki went to his house to patiently wait for her Prince Charming to arrive. Her pregnancy hormones were at an all-time high. When Lamar pulled up, she instantly got wetter, wasting no time getting his pants off once he entered the house. Nikki started to suck Lamar's dick and moan at the same time, showing him that she wanted it just as badly as he did. Then, bending over, she told him to lick her pussy. The young nigga ate that pussy like it was caviar—with cheesecake for dessert. Nikki told Lamar to lay his ass back as she climbed on top of him and started to ride his dick.

As the mailman was putting the mail into the mailbox, he could hear Nikki saying, "Baby, I love your dick, Lamar," which only made Lamar start fucking Nikki like he really did want to be with her... making her feel as if she was the only one for him.

# Chapter Twelve

A few days passed, and it was time for the funeral. Smitty could only imagine how Devin's mother felt as guilt overwhelmed him. Lamar and Y.I.C pulled up to the funeral home in a Mercedes Benz Sprinter and represented to the fullest. Even Smitty was in the van. Lamar knew he had Smitty's mind in a rumble trying to figure out who was responsible for the hit.

During the program, Nikki looked at Lamar and Mr. Craft, trying to figure out why they looked so much alike, not knowing that Mr. Craft was Lamar's father. It was Lamar's first time seeing his father and brother perform services as funeral directors. Amazed at how well they did it, Lamar began to think of the deal his father had put on the table. Upon seeing Latonya, he could only think about Sheila and Miyleriah… and how hurt Nikki would be when she found out about his other two kids.

Afterward, Devin's mother walked up to Lamar, thanking him for paying for her son's burial and having the repast catered. Lamar simply smiled at her, telling her that it was his pleasure.

* * *

Sheila was in the shower when she heard the knock at her front door. Not expecting company since it was almost midnight, she was a bit unnerved. Quickly jumping out of the shower, Sheila reviewed her cameras and recognized a face she hadn't seen in a while. "I wonder how the fuck this nigga got my address," she muttered to herself just before she heard the knock on the door again.

Sheila finally decided to open the door, and when she looked into his eyes, she said, "Motherfucking Lamar Deon Carroll, how did you find out where I stayed, and why are you here so late?"

"Are you gon' invite me in or just look at me…? Damn?!"

Sheila stood there looking at Lamar, reminding herself why she had fallen in love with the young nigga. Letting out a slow breath, she stepped away from the door, and Lamar walked into the house.

"Why are you here so late?" she asked.

Lamar acted as if the question was nothing to him before flopping down on her couch and propping his feet up. Sheila yelled at Lamar, telling him to get his feet off her furniture. Lamar started to laugh, but Sheila couldn't figure out what was so funny.

"I paid for it," he said.

"You haven't given me a damn dime since our daughter has been in this world," Sheila retorted. "The mortgage is $2,000 alone, not including the $800 for daycare I pay monthly."

Lamar interrupted her. "Let's play a subtracting game." Sheila wasn't in the mood to play any games with Lamar because she was irritated. Lamar chuckled and said, "I'll do the math myself... no problem." Sheila was now visibly angry. "You pay $24,000 a year toward a mortgage, $4,600 in daycare. All you're spending is $33,600," Lamar said before rising and going out to his car.

Sheila was confused as to what he was about to do. When he walked back in, he propped $40,000 on her living room table and told her to add it to the $250,000 he had sent her.

Stunned, Sheila said, "You never sent me $250K. So, you can save the lies, Lamar."

He then pulled out his phone and asked her if she recognized the check in the pictures. Sheila looked at it and told him, "Yes, I got it for Christmas last year. But, it was from someone named Coop."

"That's the captain of my team."

Sheila looked at Lamar in disbelief, wondering how

he was able to send her so much money. Sighing before asking him if he wanted anything, she told him she needed to finish her shower. Lamar knew how to get to Sheila, so he told her to go on... he'd wait. As Lamar sat back and turned on the television, Sheila wasn't sure what she wanted to do. Pulling her bathrobe closer around her body, she told Lamar that his daughter was in the room sleeping, so keep it down. She went back to the bathroom.

While Sheila was in the shower, she looked into the mirror frame around her as the hot water drizzled off her body. Admiring her perfect body, she started to play with herself while Lamar was in the living room—moaning as her fingers went in and out of her pussy. Lamar knew it had been a few years since he had fucked Sheila, so he figured it was the perfect timing. Entering the bathroom, he got undressed.

Sheila never noticed his presence until he opened the shower door. She smiled and asked what was taking him so long. Before she knew it, she found herself booted over in the shower as they both watched in the mirror. Sheila wanted Lamar to herself, which reminded him of the reason they had stopped talking.

After the two were done fucking, Sheila insisted that Lamar stay, so he did.

The next morning, Nikki called Lamar, but his phone went to voicemail. Lamar had his phone on "Do Not Disturb" while at Sheila's, thinking he was safe. But he wasn't. Sheila had taken a photo of them lying up as Lamar was asleep and posted it on her Snapchat. That photo alone had been screenshot almost 1,000 times because it was rare that anyone posted a picture with the young king. The picture had gotten back to Nikki; she was boiling hot and in her feelings.

After Lamar woke up the following day, he walked into the living room and saw his daughter playing with her dolls as Sheila prepared breakfast, thinking she had finally gotten the Lamar she always wanted. Lamar sat and played with Miyleriah while they ate breakfast. He began thinking about leaving his kids behind without a father. Sheila still couldn't figure out why it had taken Lamar so long to come around, but she was glad that he had.

Lamar got up and started to hold his daughter as she was falling asleep and went and laid her down. He then told Sheila it was time for him to go as he headed for the door; he grabbed her, palmed her ass cheeks, and gave her the kiss of a lifetime.

Just as he exited the house, Nikki had tried calling Lamar again and was surprised when she got an answer. Her words to him were, "You low down dirty mother-fucker... you been too busy laid up to answer the phone!" Lamar had seen the picture already. Since he was such a playa boss ass nigga, he only told Nikki that the picture was before her, which she couldn't dispute.

Lamar was headed back to town when Neiko called thanking him for the opportunity because he was starting to move an extra 100 pounds a month. Lamar was a boss. He took things into consideration when they were said. After making it home, Lamar decided to get some rest until he had to go out later that night.

* * *

Ms. Carroll went to visit Aaliyah and decided to catch up with Denise. Denise told Ms. Carroll that she had wanted to tell her about them, but it was Lamar's idea not to. Ms. Carroll started wondering if more kids she didn't know about existed.

"Can I ask you something?" Denise asked.

Ms. Carroll nodded.

"This isn't easy to say, and your son knows I love him. But I refuse to jeopardize what I've worked so hard for just to be with him. If he was to let the streets go, I wouldn't mind waking up to him every morning. He's at a point now that he will not let go."

As the two watched Aaliyah play, Ms. Carroll told Denise she would talk to Lamar because she had seen the woman that Denise could be.

* * *

*Pow, pow, pow, pow, pow, pow, pow, pow, pow*
*pow, pow, pow, pow, pow, pow, pow, pow...*

Shots rang out at Mr. and Mrs. Willow's house. It had everyone in the community dialing 911, tying up the phone lines. When police arrived on the scene, they found a victim face down with fourteen shots in his body. Detectives cased the scene but couldn't find any evidence —not a footprint, gun shell, nothing. Things had gotten so bad that Rayville's toughest gangsters were scared to exit their homes. Lamar had struck again and was steadily laying them down one by one.

Returning home, Lamar received a call from Smitty about the young hustler, Tony, that had been fatally shot in his parent's yard, just like Devin. Lamar told Smitty that he would be there soon and not to worry. At that moment, Lamar knew his plan was working out just fine, and there wasn't a soul who was going to stop him. Lamar then arrived at the scene as Smitty walked up to his car to meet him.

"Man, somebody is targeting my team," Smitty said, "and I don't know who it can be."

Lamar looked at Smitty and told him he shouldn't have made enemies. The two started to walk up to the Willows' house, and as they entered, a lady noticed Lamar and told him it was a good thing he had done by paying for Devin's funeral. Lamar looked at the lady and told her Devin was considered a friend, just like Tony. He then looked at Mr. and Mrs. Willow and told them he was sorry to hear what happened, but if they didn't mind, the funeral was on him. The Willows cried and thanked Lamar at the same time.

After exiting the house, Lamar told Smitty, "Whoever you got fucking problems with, you need to fix it cause you causing me fucking money."

Smitty couldn't figure out who he had problems with, and being that he sent the hit on Lamar, Lamar wasn't acting differently toward him. He figured it couldn't be him. Lamar then called his father.

"You have a pickup in Rayville at 308 King Drive... a boy named Tony Willow," he said before hanging up and telling Smitty that he would catch him later.

When Coop heard what happened, he knew it was Lamar's work.

The morning after the murder, Ms. Carroll was up at 6:30 with her coffee, waiting for the 7 am news. When it came on, the reporter said:

Another murder occurred in Rayville in less than a week. Detectives are saying they believe that the two murders are connected. Twenty-six-year-old Tony Willow was fatally shot fourteen times while walking in his parent's yard. Neighbors said when the shots started, they seemed to have never ended. The Richlend Parish Sheriff's Office asks if anyone has information about the murders to feel free to call them.

Ms. Carroll dropped her head as Lamar walked into

her house. She couldn't understand why her son was on a murder spree the way he was.

Lamar was in the kitchen, where he received a phone call… and from the tone of his voice, Ms. Carroll knew it wasn't good.

# Chapter Thirteen

Tony's funeral had passed, and Nikki was now well into her third trimester... three months away from having her first child—Lamar's third.

While the community was coping with losing one of its own, Lamar was dealing with a pressing problem. He had hired a private investigator to look after LaLa because he felt something was wrong. He had spoken to LaLa days before the funeral, and during their conversation, she started to cry but wouldn't say what the issue was.

When Lamar met with the investigator, he learned that LaLa had been working at a convenience store and stripping at a local club to pay her way through school. She didn't have a car, so her only transportation was the bus. Lamar also knew growing up that LaLa's parents weren't financially stable, but they were good church-going people who wanted nothing but the best for their daughter.

After Lamar got the news, it seemed as if his whole day went blank. Needing some time to himself, he called Coop and told him to run things while he was gone. Then, the young hustler boarded a private jet—without any luggage— and headed to Cali, where he would meet with the Godfather, as everyone called him, the Black "Scarface."

The Godfather's name was Frederick Williams, and Lamar looked up to him as if he were his own father. When the two got into the car, he asked Lamar how business was treating him. Lamar told him he was recovering from the shooting, but business was great. The Godfather knew something was bothering him because Lamar was making this unexpected visit to see him. The car had come to a stop, and The Godfather told Lamar he wanted to introduce him to a person, and if something were to ever happen to him, this was the person to call.

The two men walked into an Italian restaurant and went directly to the back, where they saw a guy sitting at a desk. The fat Italian's name was Antonio, and you could tell he wasn't the type to fuck over or have any problems with.

"If I need love, I find women, but I deal drugs, so I need Benny," the older man said.

Antonio knew precisely who he was asking for, so he

turned around, got up to greet The Godfather with a hug, and asked him who the kid tagging along was.

"This here is Lamar; he basically runs North of Louisiana. And I know you're probably wondering why you never met him until now. Well... I look at him like a son, but I figured it was time for him to meet you in case he ever needed anything."

Antonio sat his fat ass on the edge of his desk and asked Lamar whether he had ever seen a dead body. Lamar looked at him with a killer's grin. Then, Antonio asked Lamar if he was packing. Lamar pulled out his .40 cal. Smith and Wesson and said, "This one got a few bodies on it."

Antonio looked at The Godfather and said, "You should have been brought this kid around... I like him already." Then, shifting his focus back to Lamar said, "If you accept my friendship, I have a gift for you."

Lamar looked at him and said, "Okay then."

When Antonio told the guard to get the blue briefcase, Lamar gripped his pistol and went on high alert, but when Antonio noticed it, he said, "Family doesn't kill family," letting Lamar know he was now considered family.

Upon returning, the guard opened the briefcase containing a Glock .40 and $100K in cash and gave it to Lamar with Antonio's business card. The Godfather stood up and told Antonio they would be in touch as they exited the room. Although Lamar's mind wasn't really on anything but LaLa at the time, knowing he had to do something, he was keenly aware that he was about to be tied into a family of nothing but bosses.

While Lamar was making boss moves, Coop was also. Coop took over a hustler's spot in Oak Grove, but the thing about this hustler was that he was white and dealing meth. Coop kept everything running as he knew Lamar would want him to.

Neiko had met with Coop for lunch to tell him about the loss he had taken, explaining that he had taken a loss of seven pounds and replaced the money out of his pocket. Coop realized Neiko was a loyal ass team player who would rise to the top quickly. He told him to keep doing what he was doing; it was going to pay off soon.

The next day, while LaLa was at work, a man drove up to a gas pump and exited the car. Toward the end of her shift, she noticed that the car was still sitting in the same place, and the guy was nowhere in sight. So, she called the police. Three units would arrive and surround the car, only to find a note that said, "LaLa, you're welcome."

Police asked for her name, and she told them,

"Lakhia." Another officer asked if she was known by anything else, and she said LaLa. When the officer had her walk out to the car with them, she thought she had done something wrong, but they just showed her the note. Immediately thinking Lamar had done it, LaLa called him but learned he was still in Cali. So, she began to think hard about who else could have gotten her the car of her dreams.

Closing up, LaLa left the store, heading to her next job, the strip club. After getting off from a long day of work, she opened her laptop to make a payment for her tuition, only to learn that someone had paid it off. LaLa stayed up all that night wondering who had given her a car and paid her tuition, but she wasn't sure who it could've been.

* * *

The Godfather didn't have any kids, so whenever Lamar came around, he would splurge on him like he was his son. On one such encounter, Lamar told The Godfather the real reason he had made the unexpected visit.

"I came out to clear my mind with everything I have going on. Honestly, I think I have a good heart, but I refuse to be fucked over."

"My boy, listen...," the older man replied. "With this game, you gon' go through trials and tribulations. Hell, you gon' go through that in life no matter what. It's on you to continue the fight and never fall. Whatever it is you're going through, pray about it. Even gangsters' prayers get answered by God."

Lamar was speechless. The two were in the car heading toward the mall when The Godfather told the driver to go by his lawyer's office.

While sitting in the lawyer's office, The Godfather glanced over at Lamar and said, "My house is worth $3.5 million, and my cars are worth almost $7 million."

Lamar didn't know why he was being given that information; he just knew that the information would be valuable. The lawyer came in, shook hands with The Godfather, and sized up Lamar.

"You must be Lamar."

Lamar looked at him, trying to determine how he knew his name. The lawyer then told the two to follow him back to his office. The Godfather told his lawyer that he needed the paperwork for Lamar to sign before he left back out of town. The lawyer then pulled out a folder and gave Lamar some papers. Lamar looked and asked what this was about.

The Godfather then told Lamar, "I won't be around forever. I'm not married nor have kids, so someone has to be left with everything I own."

Lamar asked him if he was sure about leaving it to him. He told Lamar if he wasn't sure about anything else in life, he was sure about this. Lamar then signed the papers and returned them to the lawyer before telling

The Godfather "Thanks" and that he needed to get back to Louisiana to handle some business.

On the way to the airport, Lamar told The Godfather, "I've always looked at you like a father, and it's crazy that I've only known you for four years. When your mother died, I came to the funeral to support, and it turned out that I met a great man. I have two kids in the world and one on the way. I'm far from perfect, but in my own way, I'm different."

The Godfather waited a few breaths before responding. When he did, he said, "You alone are a good young man, but being a father will make you an even better man."

They arrived at the airport beside Lamar's jet when he got a call from Sheila asking to see him. He found it strange she called, but he told her he would make his way there once he landed.

"Sounds like you need to be boarding that flight, my boy," The Godfather said, smiling.

After Lamar boarded and got seated, the jet took off. Once they had reached their cruising altitude, he started to imagine a life with everyone and how it would be. He figured being with Denise, he would have to get out of the game entirely and cut off a few friends. He knew he would have to be more settled than he was to be with LaLa. And, being with Sheila, he could only picture them on the road a lot because she loved to travel. It wasn't a question when it came to Nikki. He knew they'd be two unstoppable bosses if they were together.

Following those thoughts, he pulled out his phone, looked at a picture of LaLa, then lay back to rest for the remainder of the trip home.

# Chapter Fourteen

**M**eanwhile, Latonya had picked up Miyleriah from daycare to take her to the funeral home. As he passed by, Mr. Craft saw her playing in Latonya's office and stopped to talk to her, asking where Sheila was because she would usually come by his office to speak. Latonya told her father that Sheila was at home and that she had picked Miyleriah up to spend some time with her niece.

"It's good that you consider your friend's child to be a niece, which says a lot about you," Mr. Craft said.

"Well, she's your granddaughter, so you should be glad I went to get her."

"What are you talking about?"

Latonya wasn't the type to sugarcoat anything, no matter who you were or the situation. So, she told her father that Miyleriah was Lamar's daughter.

"Stop playing. Lamar didn't even know Sheila!" Latonya smiled and picked up her phone, showing him the text messages between the two.

\* \* \*

Coop steadily made moves and held everything down. Then, one day, an unexpected visitor knocked at his door. He peeped out the window to see Lisa Davis standing at his door in her raincoat as the rain came down harder. He opened the door and invited her in, wondering what made her come to his house.

Lisa had cooked Coop something to eat and catered to him as if she was his ol' lady on the regular. Coop didn't know what he had done the night he went to that motel room. So, he asked if something was wrong because she had come over in the rain. Lisa looked at Coop as she was biting her lips and unbuttoning her raincoat. Coop thought she was only pulling her raincoat off, but when she dropped it on the floor and told Coop to look up, she was completely naked.

"I came to ride my man's face," she said.

\* \* \*

Lamar had just landed in Louisiana when Mr. Craft called him to come by the funeral home. He was contacting Lamar a lot more lately because he knew

Lamar had killed both Devin and Tony. Now, he found out he had a grandchild he had been unaware of. Lamar figured that what his father wanted wouldn't take long, so he decided to go by the funeral home before going by Sheila's.

After getting to the funeral home, Lamar walked in and started flirting with Chelsea—it wasn't long before he got her number. Mr. Craft heard Lamar in the front and paged him to his office over the intercom. As Lamar was walking into his father's office, he could tell that he had something on his mind that was bothering him.

"Is there anything you need to tell me?" his father asked.

"No...?" Lamar replied, unsure what his father meant.

Mr. Craft paged Latonya's office, telling her to come to his office and not to forget to bring his grandchild.

Latonya came into the office with Miyleriah, and as she was taking a seat, she asked Lamar where he had been. He told her to handle some business out in Cali. Mr. Craft told the two of them that their conversation could wait; he wanted to know why he was just finding out Miyleriah was his grandchild.

Lamar paused before answering, saying, "The same reason I'm just finding out my father is alive."

The mood in the room was immediately tense. Breaking the silence, Latonya spoke to her father. "How could you blame Lamar? He's still adapting to you being alive and not in his life," she said gently.

Mr. Craft knew Latonya was telling the truth, so he apologized to Lamar. "I wasn't there for you, son. But I will be there for my grandkids."

Lamar told him he understood where he was coming from. Latonya then asked Lamar what his plans for the future were. Would he think about going to college or what? Lamar said he would think about it, but he needed to get to Sheila's house. He grabbed Miyleriah and left without another word.

Less than two hours later, Lamar pulled up to Sheila's in a brand-new G-Wagon truck sitting on 24s—he and Miyleriah pulling out bags from their mini shopping spree. Lamar had gotten a key made to Sheila's house without her knowledge. He didn't have to knock on the door when they arrived.

Sheila had prepared dinner and fixed herself up, anticipating that Lamar was about to give her another exciting night. But to her disappointment, he simply walked in, kissed Miyleriah goodbye, and told Sheila he would see her later.

* * *

Coop had rolled up on Ted to see how everything was going on his end since he was new to the team and found himself in a war zone. Ted would hustle and make money, but he had trouble with twelve. The police had Ted at gunpoint when Coop arrived to beat the shit out of Elizabeth, his ex-girlfriend. Coop got out and asked the police to let him talk to Ted without the police shooting them both—so he could calm down.

Ted started yelling, "Man, the bitch is crazy. She came over here wanting to fuck, and I told the doped-out bitch no, and we started fighting."

Coop told Ted to let him handle the situation. He then walked up to the officer while he still had his gun pointed towards Ted and told him, "I want you to put your fucking gun down first thing first. Second, get on your radio, call your chief, and tell him to get his ass here with the mayor before he be less an officer."

The officer looked at Coop up and down as he heard Ted say, "This motherfucker about to get me killed." Elizabeth was on the porch yelling, "Kill that bitch." The officer started laughing in Coop's face, only taking him as a joke since he didn't call anybody until he saw the barrel of a .40 in his face. The officer got on to the radio and called for the chief and mayor to come urgently... and to come alone.

It wasn't long before both men came rolling in on two wheels wanting to know what the emergency was. And as the two men were walking up, Coop told them to stop and listen.

"You two motherfuckers come on and join the fucking party," he said. "This how this shit gon' go. My man, Ted, is gonna move ice in this small hillbilly ass town, and he gon' put y'all two sons of bitches on payroll!"

Elizabeth was still in the back screaming until Ted finally got up and smacked her ass.

Coop looked at the chief and told him, "Your deputy has ten seconds to put his fucking gun down before I pop one in the mayor."

The mayor couldn't take the shit happening, so he told the officer, "If you don't put that got damn gun down, son, your mammy won't be able to live in this town."

Coop then looked at the officer and told him he was such a good boy.

\* \* \*

Nikki was alone at her doctor's appointment and hadn't heard from Lamar in the past few days. She knew something wasn't right. She called Ms. Carroll, who thought this was strange because she hadn't heard from Lamar either. Still, they both knew if anyone was aware of where Lamar would be, it was Coop. So, after the two hung up, Ms. Carroll called him to get a location on her son. Knowingly, he was so loyal to her son that she knew it would be a waste of time.

\* \* \*

Lamar was finally able to swing by Coop's house to check on him. Pulling up, he saw Coop's car backed in, which was very strange. He knocked on the door, and Lisa answered it—in a bathrobe. Lamar thought to himself, *This Nigga ain't shit. He got this man's wife up in here damn near living here.*

Lamar walked into the living room as Coop came from the back. When Coop came out, he kissed her and said, "I'll be back," as he and Lamar walked out the door.

Getting into the truck, Lamar didn't let up. "You mean to tell me your tricking ass trying to be in a relationship with her? Wait, then she married?"

Lamar was laughing, but Coop wasn't. "I been making moves, unlike your missing-in-action ass. I added a new member to the team, so we have now taken over Oak Grove territory."

"What you mean you added somebody to the team?"

"Nigga somebody had to be added to take over that area. I'm already running two areas alone."

Lamar kept driving and told Coop, "Well, we about to pay this nigga a visit... *Boss.*"

The men pulled into a trailer park once they had made it to Oak Grove, seeing nothing but white people. Lamar asked Coop if he was sure the nigga lived down here. Coop told Lamar to drive his ass on down the road. They made it to a trailer with shit all over the yard and windows boarded up.

"You better hope this nigga isn't twelve," Lamar said.

Coop nodded, called Ted, and told him to come outside. When Ted stepped out the door, Lamar told Coop to stop playing with him.

"What... you ain't never seen a white hustler before?"

"I'm going to kill you and this motherfucker," Lamar replied, getting out of the car, shutting the door, and walking up to Coop and Ted to be introduced.

"Are the connections I gave you working?" Coop asked.

"Working is an understatement... it's booming!" Ted replied, grinning.

"You got your mayor and chief of police on payroll yet?" Lamar asked.

"Thanks to Coop almost killing them, yeah, they are on," Ted said. "I feel like I'm working for the best man around. I been heard about you, and I know by being on your team, I'm going to make a lot more money!"

"Everyone on my team is a hustler, so consider yourself a team member," Lamar replied. "Welcome aboard."

Lamar and Coop headed back towards the truck, but Lamar didn't do nasty or like being in that type of environment. Turning around, he told Ted to fix his house and yard before getting in the truck.

# Chapter Fifteen

"The more I think of you talking to that guy Lamar, the angrier I get," Montrell, LaLa's boyfriend, said.

LaLa met him in college, and the two quickly engaged in a serious relationship. Montrell was a starter on the basketball team and destined to go pro. Montrell had just come from basketball practice and was hanging out at LaLa's apartment until she left for class. He was curious about how she had gotten a brand-new car. A good guy in front of others, he was an abusive boyfriend behind closed doors. At times, LaLa would have to use makeup to hide the bruises.

While the two were chilling, her phone rang. She looked over to see who it was, only to ignore the call.

"Who was that?" Montrell asked.

"Nobody..."

Glancing down at the phone, he saw a missed call from "Daddy General" and started to slap LaLa. "Bitch!" he immediately exclaimed, now choking her. "Why you lying to me?!"

* * *

Ms. Carroll hadn't heard from her son in about a week. *With all my son's killings, I hope nobody has killed him.* Her nerves were all over the place, but she couldn't file a missing person report because of Lamar's run-ins with the police. The more Ms. Carroll worried about her son's whereabouts, the more she learned she wasn't the only one.

Nikki was also worried since, along with not coming to the pre-natal checkup, Lamar hadn't even called to check on her. So, she decided to go by his house to check on him. His car was in the driveway when she arrived, so she figured he had to be there. But no matter how much she rang the doorbell, there wasn't any movement.

Lamar had a security system to alert his phone when someone came onto his property and record their every move, so he could see Nikki at his door. Aware that she wouldn't have any idea that he had bought a second vehicle and wasn't there, he still chose not to respond. At that moment, Coop was getting out of the Benz truck when Lamar told him to close the door for a second.

"I'm proud of you, boy," he said. "You done stepped

up and showed me the reason I made you team captain. Keep making the moves you're making. It's all gon' pay off, I promise."

Coop looked at Lamar, thanked him, and exited the truck. Lamar then hit the interstate, still not going to see his mother. His mind was on the problem he needed to eliminate.

Later that night, the streets of Rayville were so quiet you could hear a mouse running through a tunnel. At least until 03:14, when shots rang out directly behind the police station.

As officers raced to the scene, they didn't find a car nor see one, but they found a body slumped over in the middle of the road with fourteen shots plunged into him. The detectives knew that whoever the murderer was loved the number fourteen or had a distinctive trademark on how he left people. The town had gone two weeks without any murders and two weeks without any stress believing that whoever committed the last two murders had left town.

Smitty called Lamar and told him what had happened, but Lamar only gave him his father's number. The young hustler, Carter Kales, was known to stack his paper and move swiftly, but his funeral was already paid for in advance. When Smitty arrived, a detective noticed he had been at the last two scenes and wanted to speak to him. However, Smitty declined the offer to go downtown to talk due to the fact that he knew Lamar would find out. Instead, he called Mr. Craft and gave him the information about Carter so he could pick the body up.

After pulling up to Carter's mother's house, Smitty showed his respect to her while sharing that a friend had already paid for the funeral. Smitty still didn't know who was coming for his team, but he knew it wouldn't be long before they came for him too.

\* \* \*

The following day, Ms. Carroll had prepared her coffee and sat back in her chair, waiting for the news to come on. Breaking news was the headline:

Another murder has taken place in Rayville.
Police say Carter Kales was gunned down right
behind the police station and shot fourteen times.
Just two weeks ago, two victims were murdered...
also shot fourteen times. Police are saying they
think all three murders are connected somehow.
The Richlend Parish Sheriff's Office is asking if
you have any information regarding the three
homicides, feel free to give them a call.

Ms. Carroll was relieved to know her son was alive,

but she couldn't understand why he was doing all of this killing.

* * *

Nikki had begun to stress herself out from the distance of Lamar. When she heard a knock at the door, she grabbed her gun and went to see who it was. Peeking out the windows, she saw a candy yellow G-Wagon. Not knowing who it was, she was prepared to shoot. Only after hearing Lamar call her name she opened the door. Seeing him, her stress immediately disappeared, but her anger increased.

Lamar walked in and sat down like nothing was wrong as Nikki stood behind the door staring at him. "What do you want, Lamar?" she asked. "Because you haven't called and checked on me for over a week!"

Lamar stalled her, saying, "Damn, Jr., Father can't get no love."

Nikki wasn't about to take Lamar's shit. "Nigga, you must think shit all gravy with us. You been out here fucking bitches left and right, and I'm at home worried about you being safe. You got bitches posting you on Snapchat talking about they baby daddy done came home, your mama didn't even know where you were, and Coop's big ass wouldn't tell nobody nothing. Mother-fucker... you got some nerves, bitch."

Lamar had never seen Nikki act this way before, so

he thought before he responded. He looked at Nikki and asked her to sit down, but she was too mad to sit. "I've been out of town handling business and making new friends—not female friends—connection friends. You are tripping over a picture that I told you was old. Matter of fact, we already had this conversation before. Coop didn't even know where I was, and I know you been by my house. I saw you from my phone, so calm down, please... and go get dressed."

Nikki gave Lamar a look she would usually give people, the look of a killer, but she did as he asked. While Lamar waited, his phone began to ring as LaLa's name popped up on the screen; he stepped outside and answered her call. LaLa asked if he had a second to listen to her. He told her yes and sat in his truck. LaLa broke down crying.

"I couldn't call my dad or anyone else. All I had left to call was you."

Lamar didn't want to rush into the problem, but he sure wanted to know what was wrong.

LaLa then told Lamar that she couldn't take it anymore, "Lamar, Montrell is a guy I have been dating, and he's on the basketball team and all, but the other day he got mad when you called and started to beat on me. Then he beats me every time he thinks I talk to you. He says you were the one who bought my car, but I told him you weren't."

Nikki was walking out the door when Lamar asked

LaLa what Montrell's last name was, she told him Washington, and he told her he would be in touch. Then, he called a nigga named Kilo and told him, "At twelve tonight, I want Montrell Washington at my spot."

Since everyone was loyal to Lamar, Kilo began his hunt as soon as the conversation ended. Nikki had gotten into the truck and asked Lamar when he got it. He asked if there was a problem with him having it. Lamar knew he was pushing her buttons every time he made a smart comment; he could see the aggravation on her face. Shrugging it off, he headed toward the highway, deciding it was time to check on his mother, but the call went to voicemail. Why wasn't she answering his call?

"Your mother stays stressed out and worried about whether you are safe or not..." Nikki said. "You should consider calling her every day to see about her."

Lamar nodded as he knew she was right.

* * *

After picking up Carter's body from the morgue and bringing it to the funeral home, Mr. Craft looked at it and said, "That's three... still two to go." He then stopped by Latonya's office to see if Lamar had called, but he hadn't yet.

Latonya asked her father what was wrong because he seemed a bit distressed. He told her he had just picked up the third person out of the five. Latonya didn't understand her brother's lifestyle but couldn't believe he was a killer. Still, she knew people feared him. Calling Lamar again, this time, he answered. When Latonya asked why he hadn't returned her calls or text, Lamar stated that he had been handling business and would talk to her later. He and Nikki then pulled up to a fine restaurant for lunch.

Nikki couldn't believe that she was getting treated by Lamar since it had been so long. After they had been seated, Lamar ordered the finest shots they had. Nikki had never seen Lamar take down shots the way he was at that moment. She asked what was bothering him, but he insisted that there wasn't anything troubling him before he downed another shot.

# Chapter Sixteen

After lunch was over, Lamar decided to pop up on his mother and see her. As he pulled up, he saw that she had company. As Nikki and Lamar walked in, he spoke to his mother and introduced Nikki to Special Agent Denise Williams—though Nikki remembered Denise from the hospital.

"Me and your mother were just catching up about how far I've made it on your case and the progress I am making," Denise said. "But if you don't mind, may we have a word outside for a second?"

Lamar and Denise started for the door, but before she went out, she said her goodbyes to Ms. Carroll and Nikki. Then, once they had made it to Denise's car, Lamar began to talk but was cut off.

"Is Nikki pregnant by you?" Denise asked.

Lamar knew how Denise felt towards him and how

Nikki felt, but he never thought he would see the day that the two would put him in the position to choose between them. "Yes, that's my child... but Denise, be real. Before I got shot, being with me wasn't even an option for you. You have always let me be a father to Aaliyah, and I respect that about you, but being a family is something you just came to want."

Denise put her hands up in frustration, then said, "I have always wanted a family with you since the birth of Aaliyah, but how could we be together if you were choosing the streets over me? I wasn't about to put my career on the line for you only to have it taken away. Who would support Aaliyah then?"

Lamar looked towards the house and saw Nikki at the window before telling Denise they'd meet for dinner later that week and continue the conversation. He then walked back into the house and sat down, but he couldn't seem to catch a break.

Ms. Carroll let her son get comfortable, and then she told him, "You ain't about to bring your ass up in here and put your feet on my furniture when you can't even answer the phone for your own mother, Lamar... where the hell have you been? I've been worried sick about you."

Lamar knew his mother was concerned, which was probably why Denise was there. So, he shared with her that he had met with The Godfather out in Cali to take care of some business. Ms. Carroll knew exactly who

The Godfather was and that they were plotting something if the two of them met up.

Lamar's cell phone vibrated, letting him know he had received a text from Kilo.

*Got eyes on Montrell. @ his dorm*
*for the last few hours*

Lamar asked his mother to give Nikki a ride home and rushed out the door, calling Coop to get ready.

As Ms. Carroll drove Nikki home, Nikki asked whether she thought Lamar and the special agent had something going on besides the case. Ms. Carroll knew her son had a child with Denise, but she wasn't the one who should tell Nikki any of this. Instead, she told Nikki to talk to Lamar about it. Nikki deeply wanted to do so; however, since she was now into her third trimester, she couldn't afford to be upset by anything that was going on or had taken place.

Latonya was sitting at her desk doing paperwork when Chelsea walked in and asked if she could speak with her. "Would it be a good or bad thing to date your brother?" she asked. "Because my feelings are only getting stronger."

Latonya was very straightforward and uncut with

anyone about anything. Setting her pen down, she said, "If you want the truth, here it is... My brother is not the typical guy you can meet and fall in love with. He's not the type that you can see a future with. But if you want a thuggish nigga just to protect you and fuck you, well... you have Lamar. Just keep your feelings out of the situation."

"Thanks for the advice, but it's killing me to know I can't have him to myself."

Latonya picked her pen back up and told Chelsea to fall in line with the rest of them.

$$* * *$$

Lamar and Coop were almost near the campus when Kilo called, telling them Montrell was headed toward the cafeteria with two other guys. Lamar told Kilo to stay on his trail and not let him out of sight. Seven minutes later, Lamar was pulling up, and it wasn't good anytime he and Coop were together to handle a problem.

Kilo walked up to the two men when he saw them and said, "The nigga got a maroon jumpsuit on with some number nine Jordan's sitting across from the grill."

That was all the information Lamar needed as he walked into the cafe with Coop behind him. They acted casual, went through the serving line to get food, and then sat at Montrell's table as if they knew him.

"Do you clown ass niggas mind if we eat alone," Montrell asked as the other guys with him laughed.

Lamar and Coop were unfazed... just watched him closely for a moment before Lamar pulled out his phone, scrolled to a picture of LaLa, and slid it across the table. Montrell acted as if he had just seen a ghost show up and slap fire from his ass. Lamar said, "I have a few requests, and you gon' do them. But first things first... act normal, get up, and get into the backseat of the candy yellow G-Wagon sitting outside."

Not knowing what else to do and realizing that he really didn't have a choice, Montrell did as he was told.

Lamar threw Coop the keys and told him to drive as he entered the truck's back seat with Montrell. "Do you need your hands to play pro basketball?" After a few seconds of shocked silence from Montrell, Lamar laid it out for him. "See, I received a call from a young lady I care for, and she was crying... meaning *her* problem has become *my* problem."

Montrell had heard that Lamar was a mob boss but now knew that Lamar had no problem handling business himself. He started to say something, but Lamar cut him off.

"Nigga... did I tell you that you could talk?! What if I was to go beat the fuck out your mother? How would you feel about that, or would you even care?" Lamar said through gritted teeth. "The difference between you and me is that I care. So, this is what you gon' do... call LaLa and apologize. Let her know that you're removing your-self from the relationship... and if I ever hear you say anything else to her, I'll put a bullet through your fucking head!"

Lamar then told Coop to stop as he told the stupefied Montrell to get out of his fucking truck before he ended up dead. Then the two got back on the highway and headed toward town.

* * *

Carter's funeral was only days away, and Smitty was becoming increasingly distressed as time passed. He knew whoever had taken his team out would eventually come for him. While sitting at home, Smitty noticed that his son was using a second phone, brand new out of the box. He asked his son where he got the money to buy the phone and learned that Lamar was trying to recruit his son.

Smitty's son had been hanging out with the Y.I.C., and he was wondering why. So, he texted Lamar that they needed to talk, but Lamar only responded that they would—at the funeral.

Lamar was meeting with some people who were wondering how the jail was getting flooded with ice and they weren't getting a cut. It then came to Lamar that Ted wasn't only supplying the streets with meth, he was supplying the jails too. He agreed to pay the warden two bands a month. As soon as the meeting was over, he called Coop to congratulate him on adding a savage-ass hustler to the team.

It was the night of Carter's wake, and The Godfather was in town to visit. As the two of them entered the church, many stood up as they walked by. Everyone knew The Godfather from his younger days, but nobody had seen him since his mother passed years ago. And now that Lamar was rolling with him, people knew where he had gotten his motivation to run and take over the streets.

They both paid respect to the dead hustler's mother and viewed the body as Lamar stood there like he hadn't done anything. Police were in force because the church feared something would happen again since nobody knew who had committed the murders—they watched Smitty like a hawk.

Smitty walked up to Lamar and asked if they could talk outside. When he started speaking, there was some shade to his tone. "I don't want you hanging around my son, nigga. You ain't his daddy... I am."

Lamar patiently waited until Smitty was done, then said, "Bodies are dropping weekly like bombs. Your whole team has been wiped out. But you still have time to count your days before you see the pearly gates, my brother."

# Chapter Seventeen

The morning was cold, the streets were wet, and Lamar's wrist was dripped out in pure gold. Detectives watched Lamar's every move, taking pictures of him as he went to every location.

Thanksgiving was coming up, and the Bayou Classic in New Orleans, which Lamar had not missed since he was old enough to go alone. Lamar and Ms. Carroll met at the Mexican restaurant for lunch when he asked her to attend this year's game with him. Ms. Carroll knew there was a lot of trouble in New Orleans, especially on Bourbon Street, and they would make their way there.

Lamar had promised Shanterrica months earlier that he would fly her out to spend some time together. But with all that was going on, he hadn't been able to get to it. So, he called and told her he was going to pay for her flight to NOLA for the weekend if she wanted to join him. Shanterrica couldn't wait to see Lamar. So, she accepted his offer.

While waiting on the food, Lamar asked his mother did she mind if they had a guest to join them. She told him long as she was respectful. Nodding, he switched to another topic. "Why did Denise come by?"

"Women have feelings, Lamar," his mother replied. "You can tell the real ones from the fake. I'll be lying if I said Denise's feelings are fake for you. But again, she is a young lady who has accomplished a lot. And, whether you like it or not, she doesn't need your money to take care of Aaliyah… the amount you give her every month is about the same as she earns on her own in one check."

Lamar didn't know what to say as he looked at his mother, thinking about Denise at that moment.

After lunch, he went to the hardware store to place an order for that upcoming Saturday. Knowing that the police were watching him, he was mindful of the way he was moving. Walking into the building, he told customers to get out and shut the door behind them. Timothy O'Neal was the hardware store's owner and a known buyer from Lamar. When the "Big Tim" store was about to go bankrupt, he had called Lamar for a favor to keep the doors open.

Lamar gave Tim a picture of Smitty's last hustler and told him he wanted him dead Saturday night. Tim knew Lamar was serious, so he made a call and passed the information along as Lamar listened to the confirmation of the ordered hit.

After leaving the hardware store, Lamar called Coop and told him that he was sending everybody out of town for the weekend, including Smitty. He would get a private jet to fly the team out to the "A" and cover all the travel expenses.

"Why, out of all the weekends, are you sending us out of town *this* weekend?" Coop asked.

Lamar didn't hide much from Coop. So, he told him, "Bro, some shit is about to take place, and I'm making sure my team is nowhere around... even me."

Lamar didn't go into details about what was about to take place. But, Coop knew whatever it was, it would be major and that Lamar was smart enough not to get jammed up.

Aaliyah had been asking to see her father. Reluctantly, Denise decided to call Lamar, having had nothing to say to him since their last conversation at his mother's house. When Lamar answered the phone, he tried throwing a joke in by saying, "I knew my baby was gon' call me soon." But he got offended when Denise told Aaliyah, "Your father is on FaceTime." He couldn't believe that the woman he made his first child with was acting differently towards him.

Lamar spent a few minutes talking to Aaliyah and afterward trying to speak with Denise, but she only blew him off.

* * *

Wednesday had come—the day before Thanksgiving. Lamar started to move around early to get things done the right way, purchasing Shanterrica a first-class ticket to New Orleans. Then, he met up with Coop. Although Coop was listening to everything Lamar was saying, his mind was elsewhere.

"What's going on?" Lamar asked.

"I was just thinking about how I was gon' play my plan out with this nigga wife."

"I thought you were playing about that with your married women-loving ass!"

Coop's phone began to ring, and it was a number he didn't know. He answered it and put it on speaker. Coop and Lamar knew who it was as soon as the voice came across the phone… it was Jasmine.

"I've been thinking after we got done texting last night, it's been a minute since this pussy done got beat up. So, I need it done. Can you handle that?"

Coop grinned and said, "I wouldn't have come to you if I thought I couldn't. How about we make it happen in the 'A'?"

Shortly after the call ended, the two men went their

separate ways. Lamar then called a guy named Ron, who owned a restaurant that was famous for smoked meats. He told Ron that he wanted food catered for four people for Thanksgiving and would be by later to pick it up.

As it was a day away from Thanksgiving, Latonya called Lamar to invite him over, but she knew how the brother rolled. The more she tried to get close to him, the more she seemed to push him away. Latonya wasn't the typical sister. Before she had learned that she and Lamar were siblings, they used to text on and off. However, Lamar seemed to have forgotten who she was.

Coop had finally come up with a plan on how he was going to fuck Jasmine. He texted her:

*When we go to Purity City this Saturday,*
*all the drinks and bottles gonna be on me. After he gets drunk as*
*fuck, then you can come on over to my room*

She was just as ready, so she responded:

*Nice plan, Daddy!*

Denise was in no shape or form to see Lamar. When he called and asked her would she and Aaliyah join him and his mother for Thanksgiving, she couldn't resist.

* * *

It was Thanksgiving Day, and Denise and Aaliyah had made it to Ms. Carroll's house early that morning... around ten. When Denise walked in, she noticed that Lamar wasn't there; neither was there any cooked food. She asked Ms. Carroll if she had seen her son. Ms. Carroll shook her head because she hadn't talked to Lamar at all that morning.

Someone knocked on the door, and a red van backed up in the yard. When Ms. Carroll answered the door, she noticed a sign on the van that said "Ronald's Catering." Lamar had not told her that he was having the food catered. The two young men began bringing in coolers, asking where she wanted the food placed. While the catering was being set up, Lamar arrived and told the guys he would take over.

Afterward, everyone was seated at the table and ready to eat when Ms. Carroll asked them to bow their heads. Lamar stopped her and told her he would bless the food. Denise and Ms. Carroll looked over at each other, surprised. Lamar started by saying, "Father, I would like to thank you for my family that is here and the family that is not. I pray everyone has a good Thanksgiving and enjoys themselves in Jesus' name. Amen."

Denise asked Lamar what his weekend schedule was because she wanted to spend time with him after they had that conversation the other night on the phone.

Lamar didn't know how to tell her that he had plans. He said he had promised his mother a weekend down at the Bayou Classic. Denise understood that it was rare for Ms. Carroll to spend time with Lamar. There was no way she was going to interrupt her time.

Lamar then sent a group text to Coop, Smitty, Jasmine, Neiko, and Ted that the jet would leave at ten that night. He had booked the finest suites in Atlanta so that the team could enjoy themselves. Coop texted back to see if he could reserve a V.I.P. section for Y.I.C. at Purity City because Lit Red received so much respect in the 'A' that it was nothing for him to make a call to get what he wanted.

Balinda wanted Nikki to spend Thanksgiving with her so they could wake up early and go shopping for Black Friday sales. So, Nikki was at her mother's house lying around while Balinda and Mr. Miller were preparing the food for that day. Balinda asked Nikki if she had invited Lamar over to eat with them, but the doorbell rang when she was about to answer. Balinda had invited family and friends over to meet Nikki and to show them that she was expecting a grandchild at any moment.

Neiko had been out of town handling family business with his sister because her husband had been shot. Upon returning to town, he got back to hustling—even though it was a holiday.

Shanterrica was sitting with her family eating when

the information about her flight came to her phone. Her mother asked her what the reason for the big smile was when she told her she was invited to the Bayou Classic by a friend and that they had bought her a first-class plane ticket. Shanterrica's mother, Ms. Martin, said, "You need to tell your friend that your mother likes to travel too." After texting Lamar to ask her if her mom could join them, instead of him responding okay, he sent information for another first-class ticket.

\* \* \*

Later that evening, Denise sent Lamar a message asking if she could come back over to talk to him one-on-one. It wasn't late, so he told her he didn't mind.

When she arrived at Lamar's place without Aaliyah, she shared that she had taken their daughter to her sister's house. Then, after getting comfortable, Denise asked Lamar to relax cause the conversation was about to get deep. She then told him, "I've been thinking after we talked the other night... I have finally come up with a solution to protect my feelings. See, I know you're going to sleep with this hoe and that hoe. I wouldn't even waste my time trying to be in a committed relationship with you."

Just as Denise finished saying this, her phone rang, so she stepped outside to take the call. Lamar decided it was the perfect time to call and check on Nikki. When he called, she sounded sleepy. Lamar told her he was calling to check on her and that he was sorry for waking her. Before Nikki hung up, she told Lamar that she loved him.

Denise had come back into the house, ready to finish where she had left off. Lamar knew he couldn't win a fight with her, so he made himself a stiff drink and listened.

"All I got to ask of you now is when you are fucking them other bitches that you wrap your dick up because I want raw dick when we fuck." Denise continued. "I also want dick on demand whenever I want it. You have to make yourself available... even if I only want to suck on it."

She then stood up, asked him what was on his mind, and began dropping her pants and taking her hoodie off. Before he could answer her, she bent over and told him to fuck her like he wanted to make another life with her.

Lamar thought Denise was losing her damn mind for a second, shocked that she had come up with her "conclusions," as she called them. But he wanted to keep her happy, so he agreed to her terms.

# Chapter Eighteen

S mitty and Jasmine were the first to make it to the jet, and Neiko arrived next, bringing everybody a bag of Kush. Just as Jasmine was about to text Coop to see where he was, he stepped through the door.

Not long after, when everyone had settled into their seats, Ted finally made it. When he boarded, they stopped talking and stared at him. He was wearing shorts with cowboy boots and star-shaped sunglasses. Nobody knew who he was but Coop. Once the initial shock of his attire wore off, Neiko pulled his gun and said, "Who the fuck is this cracker motherfucker?"

Coop and Ted started laughing. Coop introduced him to the rest of the crew and told them he was a part of the team.

After the jet took off, Neiko was the first to fire up a blunt and pass it around. He asked Ted if he smoked dro.

Ted pulled out a bag of moonrocks and asked Neiko if he wanted to roll.

Neiko looked at Ted and said, "My nigga... you good with me!"

Jasmine had gotten up to use the restroom as everybody else laid back in their recliner seats. Three minutes after she left her seat, Coop's phone began to get notifications back-to-back. He thought it was Lisa, so he didn't bother checking.

It only took the jet an hour and a half to get to Atlanta from Monroe Airport. After Y.I.C. landed, a Sprinter pulled up to take them to their rooms.

**\* \* \***

The following morning Lamar was at Ms. Carroll's house around seven-thirty to drive them to New Orleans. When Ms. Carroll walked outside, she saw a six-passenger Sprinter in her driveway. Lamar still rode in style when he went somewhere. As he loaded his mother's luggage into the van, Lamar saw a Sheriff ride by and park.

On their way to the airport, Sheila called Lamar, wanting to have a sit down with him. Lamar knew that he had his hands too deep in the fire with the women he encountered.

When they arrived in New Orleans, they drove to a motel across the street from the Superdome. As Lamar and his mother walked into the motel, Lamar was met by the manager, who confirmed that his rooms were ready and hoped he enjoyed his stay this year.

"I see you just know people everywhere you go, huh? Lil hoe," his mother said. She said whatever was on her mind when she wanted to.

Lamar told Ms. Carroll he was going to take a nap until it was time to pick up Shanterrica from the airport. She could tell there was something on Lamar's mind. She walked out of his room and into hers, thinking about how she and Mr. Craft hooked up at the Bayou Classic twenty years ago and became a couple. She had been a dancer for Grambling State at the time, and he was a football player. With that type of love, it was like love at first sight.

*  *  *

Coop woke up to a knock on his hotel room door. Thinking it was housekeeping, he opened it. When he did, Jasmine came barging in, telling him, "I know we agreed to mess around Saturday night, but I couldn't help myself. My pussy steady throbbing, dripping wet… thinking about your young ass."

She squatted down and began to suck his dick while moaning as it penetrated her throat.

Jasmine was more than ready for Coop to fuck her, but she was waiting on Saturday night to come. When she started to leave out his room, she told him that he should check his phone more often. She made her way back to the room she shared with her husband and got into the shower.

Smitty was sure that when she got out, she was going to want to have sex with him, but that wasn't the case. She teased him as she lotioned her body and dressed. Her skin complexion was so bright, and the thong was fitting her ass so tight. Jasmine knew she wasn't doing it to get Smitty's attention, but she was going to make sure she got Coop's.

Everyone met downstairs around noon and went out for brunch as they laughed at Ted, who was the true definition of a redneck. The motherfucker dressed like a hillbilly for every event. Coop came down in a blue and grey Jordan jumper with matching slippers, making his dick print show off for the ladies. That only put Jasmine in more heat.

The young nigga had her mind gone.

After brunch, the crew decided to go shopping for a little while to kill some time. Coop and Neiko took Ted into a store and changed his wardrobe because he was part of a family who always tailored themselves as they should.

Smitty and Jasmine walked into Victoria's Secret, where she began to shop for the sexiest lingerie she could find. Smitty's favorite color was green, and Coop's was blue. So, she got a dark yellow set, not to make it obvious who she was getting it for. Smitty told her that if he had known she was going to dress like that for him while out of town, they would never stay at home.

While shopping, Neiko ran into a woman and her daughter and asked her if he could get a second of her time. She stopped, and Neiko asked what her name was. She told him that her name was Kaitlyn and her daughter's name was Tatiyanna. Neiko spoke to Kaitlyn's daughter first, asking if she wanted some ice cream. When she nodded yes, Neiko looked at Kaitlyn and asked her to join him on an ice cream date.

When the three of them had gotten their choice of ice cream and found a table, Neiko told Kaitlyn he wanted to get to know them.

"What do you want to know?" Kaitlyn asked.

"Everything."

"Well, I'm twenty-six years old, a single mother with a five-year-old daughter, and in school full time. I work at Purity City to pay my way through school. I love spending time with my family and taking trips."

Neiko looked at her and said, "I think I just met my wife," as the pair laughed. Exchanging numbers, he told her and Tatyianna he would see them again soon. Then, as he was leaving, Neiko turned to Kaitlyn and whispered, "I'll see *you* tomorrow night."

Coop and Y.I.C. caught a movie for that Friday and first night in Atlanta, deciding to go to a Tank concert afterward. At the concert, Coop started chatting up a female he was dancing with. Jasmine yanked on his shirt to get his attention to check his text messages. He pulled out his phone and read:

*Don't get you and that hoe fucked up*

\* \* \*

Shanterrica's mother walked into her room as she was packing to ask if she needed to rent them a car for their arrival in New Orleans. She sat beside her mother and said, "The person that bought our plane tickets will provide everything that we will need for our trip; we just have to show up."

Ms. Martin didn't know what to think but realized that whoever her daughter had become good friends with was spoiling her.

Now just minutes away from boarding, Shanterrica and her mother were sitting in the airport when her phone rang. She answered it with a smile as her mother looked at her. Lamar called Shanterrica and told her he couldn't wait to spend time with her for the weekend and that he missed her black juices. Smiling because she had gotten a Brazilian wax in preparation for Lamar and was ready to show her curves off in New Orleans with a boss, Shanterrica blushed so hard that her mother said, "My baby den fell in love."

Within a couple of hours, the two had landed. Walking through the airport, a man in a black suit stopped them and told them, "I was told to get your bags and bring you to my boss." Ms. Martin looked at her and gave her bags to the guy.

When they made it outside, they saw Lamar and his mother standing outside the Sprinter to welcome them with open arms. Shanterrica jumped into Lamar's arms and breathed that she couldn't wait to use her new tongue ring into his ear. Lamar smiled, reaching his hand out to greet her mother before introducing his mother to Shanterrica's. The moms greeted each other with love.

After leaving the airport, Lamar took the three women to get their nails and toes done. Ms. Carroll had the chance to chat with Ms. Martin, asking if she knew her son's history and whether she was okay with it. She told Ms. Carroll all she heard was that Lamar was a boss and not to be played with. Lamar's mother simply nodded her head.

Once Lamar had gotten everyone checked in, he went into Shanterrica's room, and she immediately began to get naked. Lamar started to kiss her chocolate body and fill her up with dick. It had been a minute since she had seen Lamar, and that made her want to fuck him even more. As she tried to hold back from screaming, she couldn't. She was getting pounded in and out like a mixer. After they were done fucking, she slept like a princess in Prince Charming's arms.

The next morning, Shanterrica woke up and wanted to surprise Lamar with a gift she had gotten him. As he entered the front room of the suite, she was sitting there waiting on him with music playing. She said, "Good morning," as she kissed Lamar. They both sat down and talked about how good last night's sex was, trying to catch up.

Ms. Martin and Ms. Carroll had already dressed for the game and were ready for their day when they showed up at their kids' room.

Lamar's phone was ringing, so he answered it while Shanterrica went to open the door. LaLa called Lamar and told him she had something to tell him, but it could only be in person.

* * *

Coop, Ted, and Neiko were eating breakfast when Smitty came down to join them, sitting at the table with fire and damn near tears in his eyes. Neiko looked at Coop before asking Smitty what the problem was. Initially, he struggled to find words, then said, "I've been married to Jasmine since I was nineteen, and I have never felt this way. It's like the last few weeks... I've been sleeping alone. If I touch her, she will get up and go sleep in the guest room.

Last night she got out of the shower and was smelling so damn good. So, I went up behind her... trying to set the mood only to be told that she was going to bed."

Coop asked Smitty have she ever caught him

cheating on her, and he said, "Yeah." Coop then told Smitty, "Man, it's not an easy way to say this, but she about to make your ass pay."

Neiko and Ted busted out laughing at Coop as tears filled up the wells in Smitty's eyes—threatening to fall down his face.

**\* \* \***

A few hours had passed, and it was almost time for the bands to start. Mr. Craft, who was a graduate of Grambling State and a regular attendee of the Bayou Classic was there with LaTonya and staying in the same hotel as Lamar. The pair saw him as his group was getting into the Sprinter, so Lamar asked if they were headed to the Battle of the Bands.

When they said yes, he told them to get in. Lamar had so many ties with people that he didn't need tickets. He entered the tunnel like the schools and went in the dome with seats on the field.

On the ride over, Lamar took everyone to a soul Cajun restaurant he ate at every time he came to the city. After ordering, he looked at a picture Coop had sent of Smitty crying about Jasmine not wanting to fuck him, which had him laughing too.

LaTonya was careful not to stare at Lamar—she had her own memories of New Orleans... including the one when she was almost naked in Lamar's bed a few years back, but she didn't want to cheat on her boyfriend due to an argument they had. The memory that she had almost slept with her brother was eating her alive.

It was approaching 1 pm when they finished eating, so Lamar took them on a tour of the dome. As both teams were warming up for the game, Ms. Martin asked where they were going to sit. Since Lamar was a boss, he did boss things. He had them sitting in the skybox of the dome, ready to watch the game.

During halftime, Plies had come and performed with the World Famed Tiger Marching Band of Grambling State University, and Shanterrica wanted to meet him. Lamar called someone down on the field, and moments after the performance, Plies was walking through the door.

Grambling won the game, so Bourbon Street was turned up with the GSU chant later that night. Bourbon Street was the spot to be for young and old anytime you were in New Orleans. The mothers filled up on margarita bombs and were too drunk to stay out. So, Shanterrica told Lamar that she would take them back to the hotel as he went to meet LaTonya.

When they met up, LaTonya was wearing a black fitted skirt with her hair down. He looked at her with a stare down and thought for a second. She asked him what the problem was. But, he also was thinking about the past. Lamar would look at Latonya when he was around her like he wanted to say something but wouldn't... or couldn't.

At that moment, Lamar received a text from Shanterrica telling him that he needed to get to the room ASAP and the door would be cracked. Lamar rushed to the Sprinter and back to the hotel, thinking that something had happened. When he got there, he found her lying on the bed with strawberries and whip cream on the nightstand.

When Lamar asked her what the emergency was, she said, "Lamar, you have been away from me for months... if you don't get your sexy ass over here and let me taste your dick, we gonna have a problem. I know you gon' fuck me rough, so I picked up something for you."

Giving Lamar a box of handcuffs, she told him to put them to use. Lamar wasted no time cuffing her hands and grabbing her head before he started stroking her from the back. That wasn't enough for Shanterrica; she twitched her new glow-in-the-dark tongue ring around in her mouth and told Lamar she wanted to taste his dick while he licked on her pussy.

Y.I.C. was out on the town for their last night in Atlanta when Neiko received a text from Kaitlyn wanting to see him after she had gotten off. Since she worked at Purity City, she was about to see him anyway. As they made their way to V.I.P., the D.J. announced, "All the way from the boot, we have them Youngins in Charge, aye... say Y.I.C. is in the motherfucking building."

Strippers had begun to flood the V.I.P. with bottle after bottle giving the team damn near every drink they wanted.

Coop's plan seemed to be working as Smitty was getting drunk and refusing to slow down— getting so drunk that he passed out as soon as he got into the van. Jasmine had also been drinking but more-or-less sipping, watching her husband about to make a fool of himself.

Kaitlyn approached Neiko and asked if she could get some time alone after she was off. He looked at Ted and saw that he had found a snow bunny for the night. He told her it wasn't a problem as he gave her his room info.

When the crew arrived at the hotel, Ted and Neiko carried Smitty to his room as Jasmine shook her head from embarrassment. Ted got full of them jiggers and was also ready for the arrival of his snow bunny.

Neiko returned to his room and smoked a few blunts while waiting for Kaitlyn. After she arrived, the two of them sat up most of the night talking; he invited her to come to Louisiana for a week. She accepted his offer, saying that her daughter could spend that week with her parents.

Jasmine slipped into her new Victoria's Secret lingerie and a bathing robe before knocking on the door to Coop's room. When he opened it, she slid the robe off and let him take her in with his eyes. Her titties were a high yellow, and her thighs had a vine wrapped around them.

"If you gonna look me up and down, I can go back to my room," she said, teasing him.

Not having to be told twice, he pulled her into the room, shut the door, and began sucking on her neck and breasts, leaving hickey marks. Jasmine pushed Coop back on the couch and showed him his life as she stripped for him. He picked her ass up and began to fuck her in his arms as he nutted in her multiple times. Being that they both were freaks, she decided to spend the night to get fucked some more.

Back in Louisiana, the Richlend Parish Sheriff's Office had been called out to a shooting at the local Walmart. When they arrived, they found two victims with gunshot wounds to their heads. Twenty-nine-year-old Cedric Walker and twenty-eight-year-old Erica Walker were dead upon arrival. The news spread fast about the young couple. When Smitty's mother tried to call him, she couldn't get an answer.

The following day, Lamar had gotten up at 6 am because Shanterrica's flight was scheduled to leave at 7:45. Lamar had just received the news about Smitty's hustler, but he was the one who arranged the hit, so he wasn't surprised.

On the way to the airport, Ms. Martin thanked Lamar for taking her and Shanterrica out and treating them with respect. She then told Ms. Carroll they would have to catch up again without the kids because she was so much fun to be around.

"Whenever you want to take a trip," Lamar said, "all you have to do is call."

As Shanterrica got off the van, she hugged Lamar tightly, not wanting to let him go.

Y.I.C.'s flight was scheduled to leave at 10:00 that morning. On the ride over, Smitty's mother called and told him about Cedric and his wife. He couldn't believe that his last hustler had been killed, and he wasn't there to save any of them.

As Lamar drove his mother back to Delhi, he received a call from Nikki, who was crying. After calming down enough to speak, she told Lamar the words every father wanted to hear.

"My water just broke."

# Chapter Nineteen

On December 2nd, after being in labor for thirteen hours, Nikki gave birth to Lamar Deon Carroll Jr., and after becoming situated in the room, she asked Ms. Carroll and Balinda to step out for a second so she could talk to Lamar alone.

Lamar asked Nikki what the problem was. She then told him she no longer wanted to be that person that Lamar just called his son's mother and that-didn't need protection around her 24/7 because she and Jr. were perfectly fine. Lamar was thinking to himself that Nikki was the one who had gotten protection, but he realized that wasn't the case at all.

He then asked Nikki when she was transferring rooms, "Did the hospital say anything about security?"

She told him, "No." At this point, Nikki had started

to wonder who put her and her baby in protective custody.

Coop made it to the hospital with Ted, ready to see his nephew. When he reached the maternity ward, he saw Ms. Carroll and Balinda sitting in the waiting area, so he stopped to speak. Ms. Carroll hugged Coop and asked him how he had been since she hadn't seen him in a while. He told her "the usual" and "taking care of business." She then asked about Ted. That's when Ted told her that he was the newest member of Y.I.C. Balinda stood up as Ms. Carroll introduced her to Coop and Ted as Nikki's mother.

Coop wasn't trying to talk anymore; he was anxious to see Jr., so he said he'd talk to the ladies later. Upon arriving at Nikki's room, the two men were patted down before being allowed into the room. But when Lamar saw who it was, he told the guards to stop. Coop walked in, hugged Nikki, and dapped Lamar up before he reached down to pick up the newborn. Since Coop didn't have any kids, he spoiled all Lamar's kids as much as he could.

Coop enjoyed time with Jr., but Lamar needed to speak to him alone, so they stepped outside and made it to the sitting area. "Some shit going on, and I can't put my hands on it," Lamar said. "Nikki and Jr. were put into protective custody, and neither she nor I arranged it."

Lamar's phone began to go off, and it was a text from Denise congratulating him on the birth of his baby. He thanked her and asked her how she knew. Instead of telling him, she told him he was welcome for the protection. Lamar began to look puzzled and lost when Coop asked him what was wrong. He then told Coop it was Denise who had put them into protective custody.

Coop figured it had been Denise the whole time, and this only confirmed it.

* * *

Smitty and Jasmine had made it back home, gotten settled, and began talking about their trip to Atlanta. He asked her if there was someone outside of their marriage she was comfortable sleeping with... because it wasn't him. Jasmine knew at some point they would end up having this discussion because their days were getting longer, and the conversations were getting shorter.

"I can count on my hands how many times I have caught you cheating with bitches I used to consider friends," she said. "It was times I'd be at home cooking your dinner, and you bring your ass in the house talking about you not hungry; bitch, you were ungrateful. Now you are expecting me to fuck you like you my slave owner or something. But you see, I done got fed the fuck up with you and all the lies, cheating, and heartaches you've caused. You about to pay for it and that's on our two kids. You asked if there was somebody else I was fucking, huh? Yes, it is, and matter of fact, let me text him and let him know I want some dick."

Smitty couldn't believe all that Jasmine had said. Shocked by everything, he got up and left the house, which was a mistake. The local SWAT team were prepared to breach the door just as Smitty was walking out. The detective said, "We need to bring you in for questioning, and if you are willing to cooperate, we can make you a deal."

At the station, the detective threw some pictures on the table.

"The only things I want is my attorney... and your wife to suck my dick," Smitty said, leaning back in chair and folding his arms.

\* \* \*

Coop and Lamar had gone back into the room when Jasmine called and gave them the news about Smitty. Before she hung up the phone with Coop, she asked if they could meet up later, and of course, the answer was yes. Lamar told Coop to call Mr. Sveirman to let him know what had taken place as he and Ted were getting ready to leave the hospital.

Lamar knew he had to keep Denise happy, so when she called him later that night wanting to fuck, he told Nikki that he was going go home to shower and come back later.

When he entered Denise's house, he was amazed by what she had on. He asked did you call me to fuck or make love. She told Lamar to get his ass in the room cause, at that point, he was talking too much.

Hours later, Lamar returned to the hospital like nothing had happened. Just as he picked up his son, he received a call from his attorney letting him know that Smitty was out. After thanking the attorney for the good news, he hung up and called Coop, telling him to set up the plan they had discussed regarding Smitty. It needed to be done soon.

A short time later, Coop was getting out of the shower when he heard a knock at his door, but he wasn't expecting any company. He knew Lisa would pop up, so he figured it was her. Looking over at the clock, he saw that it was ten to eight and thought to himself, *Lisa is at work by now.* He opened the door and saw Jasmine with tears coming down her face.

Grabbing her, he pulled her close and hugged her while asking what was wrong. His towel fell from around him and as they both looked at each other, Coop grinned and made a joke that put a smile on Jasmine's face. While he got dressed, she sat in the living room waiting on him. When he returned to the living room, he propped his feet up and asked her what was going on.

"I've been driving around all night, not wanting to go home. William has been beating me for the longest. I've been dealing with this for a while now, and I can't take no more."

Coop didn't know what to say at that moment, so he

grabbed her by the hand and said, "Consider your problem handled," and then stepped outside to call Lamar.

It was a cold morning outside when Latonya made it into the office. Mr. Griffin walked in behind her, showing pictures of her newly born nephew. Latonya had been feeling bad since the Bayou Classic, as guilt was eating her up. She asked her father if he could sit down for a second to hear her out, and he did just that.

"A few years ago, before I found out Lamar and I were related, I found myself in his bed, ready to open my legs."

Mr. Griffin looked at her for a moment, confused, before asking her what she meant.

"We were texting at first, then we got to New Orleans for the Bayou Classic, and we almost had sex," said Latonya.

Mr. Griffin was mad at himself for not introducing them sooner than he did. Latonya asked her father not to mention anything to Lamar because she could tell that he wasn't sure if it was her.

* * *

Denise was at work when she received a call from her friend, a detective at the Sheriff's office.

"You need to call Lamar and warn him about what's about to take place. The lead detective has gotten us together to raid his house, trying to catch him with anything. The judge is his brother and has agreed to sign off on the warrant."

Denise knew that it was only a matter of time before Lamar was arrested for something. So, she asked her friend whether she had a date yet of when it will take place. She told Denise, "No," and Denise thanked her for the information. She then tried calling Lamar, but his phone went straight to voicemail.

Denise couldn't reach Lamar when she was calling because he was just waking up at Sheila's house. He had spent the night there to clear his mind, knowing the police had been following him and that they were going to get him, soon, so he was trying to spend time with everybody before it all came down.

Sheila had just made it back from taking Miyleriah to daycare when she saw Lamar in the kitchen making himself some breakfast. They both sat around the island as Sheila told him, "Good thing I ain't have a nigga in here... you popping up like you stay here at two something in the morning."

Lamar looked at her and said, "You know not to play with your life like that in the first place."

Sheila could never figure out why Lamar would do some of the things he did. She'd just be left wondering.

"The police are on my trail," he said, "and I can't escape them. No matter how much money I pay, they still fuck with me. Soon they gon' end up getting me for something, and I'm prepared for it. I know you can take care of Miyleriah yourself, but I'm a father before anything, so I'm leaving you a hundred bands before they get to me."

Sheila lowered her head and asked Lamar why he wouldn't get out the streets and leave the game alone. Usually, he would answer her, but this time he only looked at her and continued eating his breakfast.

Lamar's phone was on "do not disturb," so he saw the notification that he had a voicemail. When he checked it, he saw that that Denise had called, but chose to get back to her later. Coop had called him three times, so he went ahead returned the call.

Coop put the phone on speaker so that Jasmine could hear and got straight to the point. "Bro, I was getting out of the shower this morning when I heard a knock on the door. It was Jasmine… with tears coming down her face."

Lamar stopped Coop to ask, "Why would Jasmine show up at your steps crying?"

Coop proceeded to tell him what Jasmine had shared with him, and Lamar told Coop to send her out of town. But before he does, make sure he got clips of them fucking, and that they would handle it later that night. When Lamar hung up the phone, Sheila asked him if that was one of his bitches he was about to save. Grabbing his jacket and keys, he told her the money was on the dresser.

Then he walked out the door.

# Chapter Twenty

Ms. Carroll was outside checking her mailbox when she was approached by two men who had been sitting across from her house in an unmarked car. The first man asked her if Lamar was in the house, and she said, "No." They were looking to catch him in any way, and she knew it.

She asked if they had a card she could give her son, but they only told her to enjoy the rest of the day as they returned to their car.

Neiko had been showing Kaitlyn around until he learned she was originally from Louisiana. While at dinner, she asked him what he saw in her to stop her and make him want to have an immediate date.

"You were like a diamond in the dust, ready to be found," he said. "Your complexion was amazing, and when I approached you, you had the most beautiful smile ever. I wasn't focused on having sex with you; you could tell by our conversations. I like you for who you are. You didn't try to hide who you were… and I respect that to the fullest."

"I have never met a man like you. You're a genuinely good man," Kaitlyn replied, "not chasing after me cause of what I have between my legs, but to get to know me, and that alone made me fall for you. So, if you don't mind, can we get home so I can put this pussy on you."

Neiko signaled for the waiter to get his bill so he could pay as soon as possible.

Later that night, Lamar called Coop and told him to come to pick him up so they could deal with Smitty. Jasmine let them in and left the house. Smitty had gotten a text from Jasmine to come home, and he figured she had gotten her mind right, ready to fix their marriage.

While the two men were waiting on Smitty, Lamar received a call from Nikki; she was checking on him because she hadn't heard from since he had left the night before. Lamar told her he was okay and would see her as soon as he finished handling some business.

Ten minutes passed, and Smitty walked in, yelling out Jasmine's name. The house was pitch black, so he turned on the lights only to find Lamar and Coop sitting in his living room. Lamar then told him to have a seat and join them while they viewed a slide show. The first slide Lamar showed was a picture of Devin's body before the police had made it to the scene.

"You see, I found out in the hospital you were the one who rented the Tahoe for your crew to take me out."

The second slide showed the crackhead he shot after the Dallas trip. Coop began to slowly screw on his silencer as Smitty watched him. Lamar then came to the slide of Jasmine making love to Coop.

"So, you tried to have me killed first, then played it off as you didn't know… and finally, your wife left you for a young nigga," said Lamar.

As Smitty tried to respond, Coop shot him seven times and the two left the house, leaving the door open for the scent to get out.

Heading back to town, Lamar gave Coop a bag and told him, "If I was to get arrested, open this, but until then, don't go in it." Then, after he had gotten dropped off and was getting into his car to drive over to Nikki's house, he decided to call Denise back. As soon as he pulled out of his driveway, he was surrounded by police cars and held at gunpoint.

When Denise answered the phone, she heard Lamar say, "They just got me."

"Lamar Deon Carroll, the nigga we wanted to see off the streets," Detective Anderson said, looking at Lamar. "The thing about catching you now is that my brother-in-law has set a million-dollar bond on you... knowing that you won't be able to make bail, your black ass won't see the light of day any time soon! I'm going to celebrate tonight."

Lamar started laughing at the detective each time he said something. The detectives in the interrogation room wanted to know what was funny so they could laugh, too —figuring Lamar was just a regular hustler who didn't know any better. But he was he was a smart hustler and knew better than them that he would get through this in short order.

After being booked into the parish jail, a guard told him, "I wish they would've killed you so I wouldn't have to look at you."

Lamar smiled and told the guard, "You still mad about me fucking your daughter, clown ass nigga."

The guard began to sweat because he was nervous being around Lamar. Once Lamar was placed into the dorm, people from all areas showed him love and respect as the young boss made his way to his bunk. A hustler named Odelle, who was from Winnsboro and a known legend, ran the dorm—whatever he said was law.

Fearing no one, Lamar was comfortable in his bunk when Odelle came into his space, standing over him at 6'5, 296 pounds. Standing up, Lamar faced him like a man and asked, "Is there a fucking problem?" But to his surprise, Odelle's agenda for this visit was different than what Lamar expected.

That next morning, Lamar made breaking news.

A known mob boss is off the streets after detectives surrounded his car last night and found eleven grams of marijuana and a duffel bag containing three thousand dollars. Police say that Lamar Carroll, better known as LilRdze Gutta, was taken into custody, and his bail was set at one million dollars. They also believe that he is connected to at least one of the murders that took place in Rayville in the past month.

Denise called Ms. Carroll and told her what had happened, but Lamar's mother let her know that she had already heard the news. She then asked Denise to come over to see what they could do even though it was late. When Denise arrived, she could tell the older woman had been up all night without any rest. She told Ms. Carroll she was sorry she couldn't make it earlier but had taken the day off to help.

The two sat around the kitchen table, considering ways to get Lamar home because they didn't know what he wanted to do. A short while later, someone knocked on the door. Ms. Carroll yelled out, "Come on..." and Coop came through the doorway, carrying a duffel bag.

Sitting it on the table, he told them that Lamar had given it to him earlier that morning, along with a letter, which he read out loud:

> *By now, they've gotten here. So this is $300K for my bail. Call my attorney, and tell him to get me. If you all have any problems, work with Coop.*

Ms. Carroll picked up her phone and called Mr. Sveirman. While she was calling him, Nikki was calling her, and so was Mr. Griffin. Since Lamar had made the headlines, it had confirmed everything Mr. Griffin had said about Lamar. He knew his son had committed all four murders, but the question he wanted someone to answer was, "Why?"

* * *

"Can we talk for a second?" Odelle asked, sitting on Lamar's bunk. "I respect you, lil nigga... you done did what most people have always wanted to do, and you weren't afraid to. I been in here seven months, going back and forth to court, trying to beat my case with a bond of half a mil."

"What you in for?"

"I was in the car with my nephew when he robbed a bank...."

While they were talking, a C.O. came over the

intercom and said, "Lamar Carroll... pack your stuff up and get to the door!"

Odelle shook Lamar's hand as he stood to leave, telling him to stay up because he had made a real nigga proud.

Mr. Sveirman showed up with a bondsman and posted Lamar's bail, but as they left the facility, Lamar turned around and told the bondsman to post Odelle's bond. After this was done, Odelle came outside to see Lamar and Mr. Sveirman standing side by side, waiting for him.

"Thank you, Man!" Odelle said, grateful.

"You got you a lawyer?" Lamar asked.

"Yeah," Odelle responded, "...a court-appointed one."

Lamar told the attorney that Odelle was now a part of Y. I.C. So, he needed his case taken care of. Since Nikki had given birth to Jr. and gotten out of the game, he decided to take some pressure off Coop and give Odelle a chance. Mr. Sveirman told Lamar that the judge set a court date for Thursday, which was only two days away. Lamar knew that since they were moving so fast, they were gon' fuck over him.

Later that day, he pulled up on Smitty Jr. because he had gotten the word about his father. Lamar told S.J. he knew he had been hustling and knew his father had Rayville on lock.

At first, S.J. wasn't following Lamar until he said,

"I'm giving you a chance to take over your father's territory and be on my team if you want it." He was thrilled by the opportunity.

After Lamar made it back to town, he slid by his mother's house and told her that if it wasn't Coop calling to find him, he didn't want to be bothered.

So, no one heard a word from Lamar until the day of court. He called Nikki and spoke with her—promising he would come home to her soon as court was over. Denise went to work that day, not wanting to go into court with Lamar because she couldn't stand to see him in that position. Sheila was on edge, scared of what would happen to her child's father.

As he and Ms. Carroll pulled up to the courthouse, his mother said a prayer, asking God to protect her only child from any hurt, harm, or danger.

When court began, the judge asked the prosecutor if he wanted to handle everything that day, but the D.A. wasn't quite prepared. Mr. Sveirman did ask the judge to consider that Lamar was a father, and if he had to do any time, he needed to spend time with his kids first. The judge responded to the attorney with a look of death—he did not care.

The D.A. asked for a continuance, saying it was too soon to have a tight case, but the judge insisted that it be handled immediately. So, the district attorney quickly looked at the police report and told the judge that he thought Lamar should be sentenced to two years in the parish jail.

"I hereby order you to serve two years in the parish jail, and next time you set foot in my courtroom, you will pay the price."

As officers handcuffed Lamar, you could hear Ms. Carroll cry out.

"Mom, it doesn't end here," Lamar promised. "I will return."

# Chapter Twenty-One

"**I**nmate 0732619... get the fuck up and get ready for visitation!"

Lamar was lying in his bunk, staring at the ceiling, when he was called over the intercom. Facing his problems like a full-grown adult, Lamar was prepared to see his mother, who had shown up for a visit.

The guards searched Ms. Carroll to ensure she wasn't bringing in anything. As Lamar walked out of his dorm, the guard gave him an evil look and said, "It's an old bitch down there waiting on you, Nigga," as he began to laugh. Trying to stay calm and not react, Lamar kept walking.

As soon as he saw his mother, he reached out and hugged her tightly, as it had been three weeks since they had last seen one another. Guards sat near them as they talked—considering Lamar a high-risk inmate and treating him as a threat to them. So, whenever they came into the dorm to do their count, they would come in threes with cans of mace.

"Ma, how you been?" Lamar asked.

Ms. Carroll couldn't keep the tears from streaming down her face. "Jail is a place I never thought I had to visit you at. Since you're who you are, I have to accept it."

Lamar had never seen his mother cry over him as she was at that moment. He knew that his lifestyle was finally catching up. As she wiped her eyes, he said, "The warden has approved weekly visitation to keep down problems. So, I'm going to use it to the best of my abilities. Next week, I need Nikki, Jr., Sheila, Miyleriah, Denise, and Aaliyah here. This is how you reach Sheila... call her at this number."

Ms. Carroll didn't know of Sheila but agreed to do as Lamar requested. "Your father and team have been asking to come visit you... so, what do I need to tell them?"

"Tell them to give me a couple of weeks," he replied, getting up. Saying that he would see her later, he kissed and hugged his mother before returning to his dorm.

**\* \* \***

The following Monday, Sheila was getting dressed for work when her phone rang. The call came from a number she had never seen before, so she ignored it. While on her way out the door, her phone rang again with the same number, but this time, she answered it.

"Hello...?"

"Yes, this is Lamar's mom, and he wanted me to inform you that this Saturday, he has visitation set up for you and Miyleriah at 10 am at Richlend Parish Detention Center."

Sheila had never met Ms. Carroll, so it was an honor to be talking to her. After Lamar's mother disconnected the call with Sheila, she sent texts to Nikki and Denise, giving them the same message.

When Lamar returned to his dorm, he was called to the flap. He wasn't just a dude from around the way; he practically ran the jail and still called shots. Another inmate had come around and asked Lamar what he wanted to eat for dinner.

"A T-bone... well done, with broccoli and rice."

Lamar's bunkmate was named Ace, and the nigga was loyal to Lamar like he had known him for years. Lamar took an interest in Ace, whose real name was Anthony, and made him his right hand. Ace had started getting the same treatment as Lamar eating the same meals as him every night.

On Friday, the day before visitation, Warden Knight

had Lamar and Ace brought to his office. When they were standing before him, he said, "I know y'all are moving drugs throughout my jail and making money... I want a cut."

Ace asked, "How big a cut you talking about?" while Lamar sat quietly. The warden acted as if he had no clue how much to demand, so Lamar told him, "You'll get ten percent if you can approve all my requests."

Warden Knight leaned back, propped his feet up on the edge of his desk, and told Lamar he was listening. Lamar then told him, "Get this...I understand this is your jail, but I'm running it... and there ain't a soul alive that's gone stop me. I'll respect all who respect me; therefore, from this day forward, all dorms will go out for yard day, and your guards will mind they fuckin' business."

"I can assure you of your request," Warden Knight said, leaning forward again as Lamar and Ace exited his office.

After returning to the dorm, Ace went around bragging about how Lamar handled the warden like a bitch.

As planned, all the women had shown up with the kids on Saturday morning. While waiting for Lamar to come out, Ms. Carroll asked everyone to move to one big table for the visitation. Lamar had just made it into the chow hall, where everyone was sitting patiently waiting on his arrival.

Aaliyah and Miyleriah were his oldest, and as soon as they saw him, they both ran toward him, screaming,

"Daddy!" which caused the women to look around...mainly Nikki. Lamar picked up his two little girls and sat on the opposite side of the table with his mother and daughters facing the three mothers. Ms. Carroll had Jr. in her arms, rocking him back and forth, trying to put him to sleep.

"I have invited you all here for one reason," Lamar began, "and that is for y'all to get along with each other for the kids' sake." Starting with Denise, he introduced her as Aaliyah's mother, then Sheila as Miyleriah's mother, and then Nikki as Jr's mother.

Each woman greeted the other warmly, but Nikki had thought throughout her entire pregnancy that she had given birth to Lamar's first child... until now. She recalled the day Lamar and Denise had stepped outside to talk, knowing that they had something going on, but there wasn't anything she could prove.

Sheila then asked Lamar how he had been doing since being locked up. Lamar began to laugh before telling Sheila, "I run shit everywhere I go. Haven't nothing changed but the place where I lay my head."

Denise looked at Lamar and told him, "You're about as crazy as crazy gets," as everyone burst into laughter.

Ms. Carroll then told the ladies, "I knew about Nikki, and I recently found out about Denise and Sheila. I'm sorry I'm just finding out about you and my beautiful granddaughter. Maybe, we can have family days with the kids and meet up to just talk."

All women agreed and waited for Lamar to finish talking as he and the girls were playing with the baby. Lamar then looked at each one of the women and told them they were to act as a family because he wanted his kids to get to know one another. All three ladies knew Lamar was serious, so they took heed to everything he said.

The guard told them visitation was over, so Lamar hugged and kissed the children, then got up to hug Nikki while whispering, "Thanks for being a rider." After Nikki left with Jr., he hugged Sheila and whispered for her to have the bed ready on the day of his release. She laughed and said, "Okay," grabbing Miyleriah by the hand.

Denise was the last to leave since she and Ms. Carroll had ridden together. Lamar told her, "I been needing to see you." Denise started to ask why but was stopped from completing her question by a kiss. He then grabbed her on the ass and told her, "You will become my wife... please be patient with me."

Denise's eyes began to well up, but before she let Lamar see her shed a tear, she grabbed Aaliyah and left the chow hall.

Ms. Carroll always got emotional when it was time to leave Lamar. As her son hugged her, she told him, "I'll see your hoe'ish ass next weekend."

They both laughed and went their separate ways.

The guard walking Lamar back toward his dorm told him that he was lucky to have all fine baby mamas, then he asked what his secret was. "The first thing you got wrong was they are the mothers of my kids... not my baby mamas. And secondly, you're not me."

Later that night, Sheila called Ms. Carroll. Lamar's mother answered, thinking something was wrong, only to find out Sheila called to get Denise and Nikki's mobile numbers. After she got the numbers, she called Denise first, then Nikki. Now all the ladies were on a three-way call together, where Sheila asked the ladies to meet up after visitation that next Saturday at Chuck E. Cheese to let the kids get to know each other. Surprisingly, everyone agreed, acting like grown women instead of little girls.

After Nikki had gotten off the phone, she wondered why Lamar had never mentioned anything about his other children. The thought that he could be hiding more crossed her mind.

**\* \* \***

Tuesday morning, after Sheila had gotten to work, she called Latonya to give her the details about Saturday's visit with Lamar. When Latonya answered the phone, Sheila began to talk nonstop.

"Girl, your brother is the real definition of a hoe. He had me, Nikki, and Denise all at visitation with all the kids. He introduced us to one another like we were siblings or something. You know... sometimes, I can't stand your brother. Then he had the nerve to tell me to have the bed ready upon his release."

"So... Lamar is cutting up really bad, huh?" asked Latonya. When Sheila answered, "Yes," she then asked if they had to talk to him through a glass because she had visitation the upcoming Saturday.

"Naw... Lamar basically does what he wants to, telling the guards what to do while we were there."

Latonya then heard some commotion at the front of the office, so she told Sheila she would have to call her back.

Lamar had started a non-profit organization for kids growing up without a father to help single mothers, who were trying to work and get a higher education. The F.B.I. had seen Lamar list his charity, and that he had stated he was part owner of Craft Funeral Home to cover himself. Latonya knew Lamar was using drug money to fund his organizations and that it was only a matter of time before it caught up with him.

That same morning, Ms. Carroll couldn't believe what she had seen on the news. Louisiana's governor was headed down to meet with a renowned mob leader being held at Richlend Parish Detention Center. Governor Eric White sent out a letter to the press:

Monsters are believed to be created under beds and are known to hide in closets, but humans are

born to walk this earth and lead by example,
especially our men.

After hearing the statement, Ms. Carroll could only
imagine how the meeting between the two was going
to go.

* * *

When Latonya saw Chelsea standing behind the federal
agent doing the talking, she knew at that moment she was
responsible for everything, and was immediately angered.
Mr. Craft walked in and quickly took over the situation,
asking the three agents to join him and Latonya in the
conference room.

After they were seated, Mr. Craft asked the young
agent what he could help him with. The agent asked if
Lamar was part owner of the funeral home; Mr. Craft told
him he was. While Mr. Craft was answering questions,
Latonya was looking at Chelsea, sitting across from her in
an F.B.I. jacket. The young man then asked Mr. Craft if
Lamar was moving drugs through the bodies at the funeral
home. That's when Mr. Craft looked at him and told him,
"My son is not a drug dealer: he's only human... well, a
young black man who's trying to make it in society."

At that, the three agents got up and exited the room.

"When is visitation with Lamar?" Mr. Craft asked.

Latonya told him that it was scheduled for this upcoming Saturday. Mr. Craft didn't say anything as he walked off, leaving Latonya in the conference room.

* * *

The next day, Governor White had made it to Richlend Parish Detention Center, ready to see Lamar. He was escorted by the Louisiana State Police, with Officer Miller being one of the escorting officers.

Warden Knight was pleased to meet the State Governor and to have him come out in the middle of nowhere to his facility. The governor was seated in the chow hall, waiting for Lamar to come from his dorm to join him.

"Lamar Carroll, it's a pleasure to meet you, young man," the governor said.

"It's an honor to meet you also, sir," Lamar replied, looking around.

As they both took their seats, the governor said, "The reason I wanted to sit down and speak with you is that the news and media have made you out to be such a bad guy... so I wanted to meet you myself."

Lamar took a close look into the governor's eyes before speaking, then said, "At the age of nineteen, I have accomplished more than people that's been living for fifty years. I don't stress over problems cause it's rare that I have them. The reason I'm sitting in jail speaking with you is that the lead detective was the brother-in-law of the judge. So, they made sure I was put away. The night I got arrested, I had a few grams of cannabis and a couple of thousand dollars on me—I was never caught with drugs, only money. They never had proof of me dealing drugs. So, I wasn't sentenced for the crime... I was sentenced because I'm black with power and money."

Governor White sat quietly for a moment as he opened a folder and spoke to Lamar about a charity that he had started.

"Oh... 'The Struggle' is my most successful charity," Lamar said. "I help kids who are unfortunate and single parents who have the desire to get a higher education.

"Well, I'm sorry you were put in this situation, but I respect you and will be considering you a good friend of mine. I'm about to go back to my office for a press conference, so be watching the news tomorrow. Thanks for meeting with me."

Lamar stood and told him, "It was a pleasure," as they shook hands and went their separate ways.

When Lamar got back in the dorm, Ace asked him what the meeting was about, but Lamar brushed him off, only telling him to stay tuned to the twelve o'clock news for tomorrow.

\* \* \*

Mr. Craft sat in his office, dialing Ms. Carroll's cell; he was in serious need of answers. She answered the phone to hear, "I know I wasn't in Lamar's life like I should have been, but I don't want to see my son dead before he's twenty-five or in jail for the rest of his life. I have spoken to him, trying to help, but he keeps telling me that all his problems are good. What am I supposed to do?"

Ms. Carroll didn't know what to do herself because of the kind of person Lamar was; he wasn't the typical youngster. He had money, power, and respect. So, she told Mr. Craft, "The only thing I can tell you to do is pray," as she hung up the phone.

# Epilogue

Coming up on **KPRD** 8 news at 12 is a live press conference from Governor Eric White. We have reporter Cameron Dominquez there at the state capitol to cover everything. Cameron?

Thanks, Jennifer. Yes, we are here waiting for Governor White to get started. From what I have heard so far, our governor had a private meeting yesterday evening with Lamar Carroll, who is being held at Richlend Parish Detention Center. Lamar was labeled as a known mob boss by local authorities and recently given a sentence of two years to serve. Back to you, Jennifer.

As we wait for the governor's arrival, we will take a commercial and return shortly.

Ace looked over at Lamar as he racked his brain as to what Governor White was about to say. Lamar was exceptionally quiet—not being too talkative about what was going on in this moment.

As Ms. Carroll sat back in her recliner, her nerves were on edge because she didn't know what Lamar and the governor had discussed. While waiting along with the rest of the viewers, she became more nervous by the second.

> We are back live at **KPRD** 8 news. Governor White has just pulled up and is about to begin his press conference. We have Cameron Dominquez live at the state capitol with many other reporters. Cameron?
>
> The governor has just stepped to the podium and is about to begin.

After a short preparation, Governor White ensured the microphone was in a good position and that he had everyone's attention before greeting those in the room.

"I'm pretty sure everyone is wondering why I called this press conference. I had the opportunity yesterday evening to sit down and talk to an intelligent young man named Lamar Carroll. During our visit, he mentioned something that has stuck with me. Lamar said that he had accomplished more at his young age than people who have lived for fifty years, which was a true statement. So, I decided to look into his files with the sentencing judge and discovered a few errors."

Ms. Carroll had begun to pace the floor and shed a tear, thinking her son was about to get more time. Inmates looked back and smiled at Lamar, thinking the same as Ms. Carroll.

The governor continued. "The error was that there was no supporting evidence to convict him of anything. Therefore, on this day, as governor of this great state of Louisiana, I will now sign this form that allows Lamar Carroll to be set free from all his charges... and order him to be immediately released from jail."

Jennifer, it seems as if Governor White has granted Lamar Carroll a gubernatorial pardon and ordered his immediate release.

Once the press conference ended, Ms. Carroll dropped to her knees and praised God. Meanwhile, the dorm was in total disbelief at what they had just heard. Ace had gotten quiet because Lamar was making sure he was straight while he was in jail, and now that he was about to leave, he didn't know what to do.

Lamar went to lie down in his bunk with his headphones, and as he heard the words, *I touchdown to cause hell*, he smiled and said, "I'm free motherfuckers...."

*To be continued in*
*Life Before and After II*

LOYALTY OVERRIDES VOICES
EVERYDAY (L.O.V.E.). REMAIN
HUMBLE AND PROTECT THE FAMILY

www.ingramcontent.com/pod-product-compliance
Lightning Source LLC
Chambersburg PA
CBHW030522020726
47494CB00004B/1201